From the Shadows

By
Keith Hearn

ISBN-13: 978-1978301740
ISBN-10: 197830174X

i

A Change

Contents

Acknowledgements

To my mum and late father.

My children Sara-Ann and Paul

I would like to thank my family and friends who have encouraged me to write.

To those who have put up with my utterings.

To my grandchildren Caitlin, Chloe, Josh and of course Bella.

I would also like to make a special mention to Caitlin and I wish her well this year as she embarks on a wonderful journey in life.

Always stay true to your dreams

I stuck to the dream of writing books

Take no notice of those who seek to knock you from your path

It took decades to make my dreams come true

Never ever give up

Keith Hearn

INTRODUCTION

This is a story about the many military veterans across the world. They have one thing in common having served their countries in so many wars and conflicts across the world

The people of Britain eventually vote for a left wing, Marxist government, who then help to bring the country to its knees. The country is hit by terrorist atrocities and up steps an ordinary man a military veteran.

The American government enforces a food blockade on the British people. NATO enforces a naval blockade around British waters.

Russia take a decision to invade Europe. Things could not have worked out any more differently almost comical.

There is so much more to read

The novel is pure Fiction

Chapter 1 – A Change

The world was by now a totally different place to how it was only 5 years previously. Many world leaders were taking their nations to the very brink of world diplomacy the world was becoming a very unstable place to live in. Some leaders had turned to social media to effect foreign policy it was a far cry from 5 years ago. In Britain the previous government successfully negotiated the country's withdrawal from the European Union. The government of the day became arrogant towards the people of Britain and they took their eye off the ball and began to think they were far better than the ordinary person and much to their cost. The ordinary person grew weary of the previous 10 years of cuts and the austerity measures. A general election soon loomed the public ended up by voting out the government and instead they voted for a left wing almost Marxist government instead, possibly to give them a chance to prove what they could do. The left-wing government in the end virtually bankrupted the country and the Prime Minister, Julien Jones wanted the country to become a Nuclear free state and a neutral country very much like Sweden. He soon opened the country to mass migration and did away with border checks and the controls, his action also allowed terrorists free and unhindered access to the country and with disastrous results. His government withdrew the country from NATO, North Atlantic Treaty Organisation including the UN, United Nations, he soon took the country backwards and back to the era of the 1970's and enforced his own ideology on the government. Russia was secretly making plans to invade Europe at the same time because of the British governments Marxist policies America was

A Change

so frustrated at the British government reluctantly placed a food blockade around the UK and NATO followed and placed a Naval blockade in International waters surrounding Britain because of the blockades, Russia shelved their plans to invade Europe. Throughout the world at the time were so many disgruntled military veterans all having served in various nations Armed Forces and they were all moaning about their own governments, not everyone is free to publicly slate their governments. At the same time across Europe many terrorist atrocities were carried out including the killing and maiming of innocent people. The British government were culpable of having funded the terrorist groups, it angered the United States and Israel. Britain through its government's policies almost reduced the Army to levels not seen since prior to the First World war the British Prime Minister ordered every Royal Navy Nuclear fleet into their ports until further notice and once again to the anger of Britain's allies. It was the kind of world people were living in at the time.

Ivor was sitting all alone sat in his spartan furnished flat in a rundown suburb of Saint Petersburg a city in northern Russia. Sitting on top of an old sideboard in the room were many picture frames of soldiers all dressed in Soviet style uniforms from a bygone era. Within a wardrobe in the bedroom and hanging on some old plastic clothes hangers were a couple of uniforms from the former Soviet Union era. Ivor had previously served with the soviet army when Russia invaded Afghanistan in 1982. He had been demobbed, from the army in 1992 soon after the Soviet Union eventually pulled out of every eastern bloc country, those eastern European counties who soon found themselves at the end of the second world war under the former soviet union's control it was only when the Soviet Military reduced the soviet military forces in those countries under the yoke of Russia all due to the consequences of the then leader of the Soviet Union Mikhail Gorbachev's "glasnost, openness" and perestroika, a political movement for reformation within the then communist party" for many old soldiers like Ivor it felt they had been discarded and thrown onto the scrap heap, just like a sack of garbage, they were no longer any use to Russian society even more so it felt to the retired military demoralising and felt worthless. Most felt forgotten about and useless most believed they still had much to give to Russian society. After leaving the army Ivor was employed in many unskilled jobs. He particularly felt Russian Society had seemingly forgotten about their sacrifice or they just did not wish to be reminded of the war in Afghanistan, or indeed what he and many of the other veterans did for the country and their sacrifices so many of them paid the ultimate sacrifice to their beloved country. He soon turned to drink to help block out the many memories and experiences whilst serving in the country and the many atrocities, carried out on captured Russian soldiers by the Taliban and of course the Mujahedeen. Atrocities were also carried out by the Soviet Troops the situation during the Afghan war ended up being a tit for tat, leading to one atrocity after another on both sides. When serving overseas Ivor was just an 18 year old conscript and it was the very first time he left the Soviet Union, never mind the city he lived in, he didn't even own a passport and had never experienced the wonders of the world. Meanwhile back in his flat he turned to drinking neat vodka it was his preferred beverage and, in his mind, he believed if he drank enough he might just be able to get a decent night's sleep? He found himself caught up in a vicious circle with no end in sight. In America there was yet another veteran from a bygone and a somewhat forgotten war and his name is Sam and he sat, in a lonely room, in a bedsit. He previously saw service with the US Marine Corps and he soon found himself fighting a war in a far-off

A Change

land the country was Vietnam at the time of his deployment he was only a 20 year old student when he was drafted to fight in a far off war, it was a war fought in the full glare of the world's press. After the war he found it extremely troublesome to blot out the violent memories including the many visions of a brutal war he found himself drinking for much of the day. He soon turned to bourbon as he thought it would help him blot out the many memories of an extremely vicious war without any success. In another country a veteran in London was also sat in a lonely bedsit his name was George and he was a veteran from the Falkland Islands war and like many other veterans across the world he soon turned to drink to help him to drop off to sleep and he used alcohol to try to block out the memories of his war? His favourite tipple was cider and he would drink gallons of the stuff. During the night when he tried so desperately to drop off to sleep he found he would continually wake up to go for a pee all due to drinking copious amounts of cider he drank throughout the day as such it had defeated the object of drinking. In Argentina there was yet another veteran of the Falklands War and his name was Lucas he returned to Argentina after the war alongside many of his fellow conscripts having been roundly defeated by British forces. The Argentinian veterans attempted to disappear from the publics gaze as most of them were so ashamed of the outcome of the war, it wasn't something to shout out about within Argentinian society. Lucas would also drink to obliterate his memories of the war. His favourite tipple was wine, and he was well known in his town for drowning out his sorrows, on many an occasion, he could be seen having been thrown out of his local bar, for either not paying his bar bill or for being legless.

Many of the war veterans across the world often found themselves unable to adapt back into society after having loyally served their country. Many military veterans will turn to drink to numb the pain of having witnessed or having experienced many horrific things some sights that others would never witness in their life time, but during his service in the armed forces he did and saw things many civilians would never be able to comprehend, and the comradery would never be found outside of the Armed Forces. Across the world there are many war veterans who find themselves sat in a bedsit or a dingy flat and every one of them dreaming of past glories with much pride in their hearts. For instance, the British government signed up to a Military and veterans convenient regarding the country's commitment to the welfare and wellbeing of military veterans, some thought it wasn't worth the paper it was written on as many veterans in their fifties or sixties would apply for job vacancies and would never receive an acknowledgment from some companies when they applied for a vacancy, even though they were more than qualified for the position. In Russia for Ivor it was worse than in Britain because his government did not have a veteran's convenient in place. Many of Ivor's ex military colleagues met up in Saint Petersburg in the various bars as it was a place where some veterans could freely reminisce about their military experiences because many of them having served in Afghanistan some thought by talking with like-minded people it went some way to help obliterate their memories of warfare and washed down with copious amounts of vodka. Perhaps they would be able to sleep in the night? But it was highly unlikely. In America Sam would meet up with his Vietnam comrades and they were trying desperately to obliterate their own memories of war just like Ivor and George over in the UK they all seemed to have much more in common, more than they could ever know. They all served with their countries Armed forces and all had some sort of drink problem and they seemed to be addicted to social media, it helped to keep them company during the very dark periods of their lives. Since having left the military each one thought their fellow countrymen had somehow forgotten about their sacrifices and for many it was the ultimate sacrifice to the country and for many survivors it ate away at the inner core they could not forgive their governments for throwing them on the scrapheap as soon as they left the Armed Forces. Each one of them no matter what country they served, thought their time would one day come again. When their government would once again call upon their military expertise. But they would have to wait a very long time as they were all living in the past and the world in the twenty first century moved on and it was a very different pace to when they last served, and it was changing from one day at a faster pace the pace of change would soon leave many of the veterans behind.

In Belgium there was yet another ex-serviceman who found himself in a very similar position as many of the other ex forces personnel and his name was Emile he also had somewhat of a drink problem and he was heavily into using social media. Emile served with the UN during The Somali Civil War where Belgium supplied many of the UN troops, during his time in Somalia the UN suffered significant casualties. He was married and as soon as he was discharged from the Army he found he could not adapt to civilian life in the end he and his wife drifted apart, his three children were by now in their thirties his wife happily remarried. Emile lived in a rundown district of Brussels. He was fast approaching his 49th birthday and had nothing to show for his life, apart from his many memories. He would often meet in the city centre with some ex-soldiers there was one man in the group, Bertrand, who would reminisce about his time fighting in the Belgium Congo in the mid 1950's he was almost 80 years old he was still sprightly and very alert, he saw service in the Belgium Parachute Regiment. In the bar was a crowd of former soldiers who would often gather at the bar and the patron who saw previous military service in the Belgium Army he would put up with the men including their swearing, foul jokes and the heavy drinking, on the days they met at his bar it would normally a quiet time mid week, they helped to bolster the pubs funds during the quite periods when the bar found itself empty. Bertrand would often hold court as previously mentioned he would reminisce about his past military experiences during his service with the Parachute Regiment everyone in the group heard his stories many times over but out of politeness and respect for him they would allow him to waffle on and whenever he spoke of his past they could see his eyes light up he would then seemingly drift off to faraway places, he spoke to them as though he was still there, in a far off country. They could clearly see how happy he was he Invoked many of his memories that he held dear to his heart and as he sat reminiscing he was sitting amongst like minded people. Back in London George was not as lucky as those who sat in the small bar in Belgium. George missed being in such company and he never visited his local Royal British Legion Club, because he thought it was far too military some members still carried their rank within the Legion and he didn't like that aspect of the Legion so stayed away. But instead he would visit his local pub and just sit in a corner of the bar keeping himself to himself, to so many in the pub he came across as a bit of a loner. The pub staff were fully aware of George because on some occasions he would leave the pub unable to walk home due to the amount of alcohol he consumed. In Saint Petersburg Ivor would visit his local super market and he would purchase the basic's such as bread, milk, eggs etc but the bulk of his purchases was vodka he knew he could so easily survive for a few days without eating any food, but he could not go a day without his lifeline, his vodka. In America Sam lost his wife a few years earlier due to an horrific road traffic accident. His two children were by now grown up and in their late thirties they were both married with children of their own. Sam's family thought he was coping very well with life? But little did they know!!

As mentioned Lucas returned to Argentina post the Falklands war in 1982 as a returning PWO, Prisoner of War and at the time he was an 18 year old conscript. He was eventually de-mobbed from the Army and he returned to his parent's house in the city of San southwest of Buenos Aires. He found it extremely difficult to readjust and most of his days were spent drinking the very cheap wine in the local bars. He tried to date the young women of the city but alas his reputation went before him. He always felt somewhat guilty for having been part of a returning and defeated Army at the time there was so much stigma felt by many who also found themselves serving in the Argentinian military, and so after the 1982 defeat Lucas had wanted to achieve glory of any kind to try and redeem himself as he truly believed there would be a time when the Argentinian government would once again call upon his military skills for perhaps one last fight. One afternoon in Belgium Emile and Bertrand were sat in their favourite bar and Emile suddenly spoke up he said, "do you know what Bertrand, I would like to do something for all the military veterans across the world" Bertrand looked at him and replied, "well you are on that bloody social media thing, can't you try to do something on it perhaps organise something"? Emile replied, "do you know what I think you might just have something there, let me see what I can do" and with that the pair carried on drinking until the early evening. Meanwhile in Saint Petersburg Ivor just finished drinking yet another bottle of cheap vodka and once again he began "surfing" on his laptop and he soon came across a Russian ex-servicemen's memories site the and following morning when he woke from his drunken stupor he continued to chat on the same site where managed to come across many servicemen who also served in Afghanistan but none of them were from his old unit it did not matter and so by the late afternoon he soon polished off almost two bottles of vodka and he became extremely argumentative while he was logged on chatting of the veterans site and he found many of the other Russian veterans who by now logged off from the site or were seemingly ignoring his posts. Life for Ivor was an existence and nothing more it seemed to be the same cycle every day, nothing ever changed, it was now his life.

In Canada yet another veteran from the first Iraq war joined the site and his name was Joe, he was yet another veteran who also found he could not adapt into civilian life after leaving the military. The Royal Canadian Legion supports many veterans and their families it does sterling work. He was married with three children but alas his world soon fell apart and he and his wife separated it is a tale well known across the world to most veterans. He too was living in a one bedroomed flat all alone. Many veterans found they all had some sort of connection with one another other not necessary a connection of nations but for veterans there seems to be a camaraderie an unbroken bond that crosses all borders. Many veterans do adapt to civilian life and do carry on as normal and make a success of their lives and careers. But there are so many who feel they have been tossed on to the scrapheap and as such feel completely useless.

A Change

The scene in many small bars and drinking dens across the world was primed for something to happen the veteran groups could be a breeding ground for extreme politics and as such were just ripe for the picking. Society would regret the decision to just ignore these very brave men and women who served their country. The scene was now set. At the same time as many of the veterans were moaning, on social media about their respective governments. Currently the political landscape within Britain was about to drastically change and not for the better. The people of Britain had recently elected a new government there was to be a massive shock to the political system regarding the election results because most of the British public unexpectedly elected a far-left government. As soon as the latest elected government took up the reins of government office life in Britain would change dramatically in many ways. The news of an extreme far left and a watered down version of a Marxist government was now running the country was, in George's mind was his worst nightmare, he knew many of Britain's institutions he believed in, would soon disappear and many other institutions would soon find themselves struggling to survive because they would not be supported by the incoming government, as the institutions were something the government had wanted to bring down it was against the leftist government's philosophy including what they had stood for and George was horrified at the thought. Even though many of the institutions leadership would have looked down at their noses at someone like George, but there would come a time when they would be grateful for people like George. Lots of British institutions were quacking in their shoes as the newly elected PM, Julien Jones together with his extreme Marxist views and his anti capitalist leanings would try to tear down the country's so-called capitalist institutions.

Having an anti-establishment government in power and running Britain had spurred George on to try and change the current political situation the country now found itself in. Even though the government was democratically voted into power by the people. The Prime Minister soon set about governing the country he was a staunch anti-nuclear activist one of the first things he did in the office of Prime Minister was to direct the Royal Navy's nuclear submarine fleet back into their home ports and to remain berthed and to wait for further instructions, his government were hell bent on decommissioning the country's submarine fleet. The minister of defence including the PM were by now drawing up instructions on how the submarines could be safely decommissioned and quickly. The decision to bring Britain's Nuclear submarine fleet back to their home ports was not conveyed to Britain's greatest and closest of allies the Americans it very soon became apparent to the Americans more so to the US Navy, as they observed that not one of Britain's nuclear submarines were seen patrolling the worlds sea's instead they were all sat idly laid up in docks around the British Isles. If it was blatantly obvious to the Americans it goes without saying, it would be blindingly obvious to the Russians. Britain's defence chiefs were acutely aware before the general election if the leftist opposition party were elected into government then the Defence of the country would be placed at the bottom of the governments list of priorities it wasn't too long before the British Defence chiefs were summoned to a high powered and senior level military meeting with the Prime Minister and the latest minister for defence and the Treasury minister were also in attendance. It would soon become abundantly apparent to all of those gathered at the conference the latest government including the PM were about to destroy Britain's nuclear capability, with the slash of a pen. The chief of the defence staff was aghast at what he heard from the ministers sat around the table and he could not contain his anger any longer because of the PM's and the defence minister's decision to keep the nuclear submarines within their home ports as far as he could tell it was to be indefinitely and the proposed reduction of the size of the Army, as far as he could tell for now anyway the Royal Navy, RN, and The Royal Airforce, RAF, would remain at their current manpower strengths. The Royal Navy had needed to keep their submariners, the crews, only to maintain the Nuclear submarines while in port. The Chief of the defence staff was politely and courteously put in his place and he knew in his mind it would be suicidal for him to remain at his post to just sit back only to observe a nation's military being reduced to a size not seen since between the two world wars. After the meeting he immediately resigned from his post and the prime Minister duly accepted his decision to resign and he wished him well in his new chosen career. There hadn't been any protestations from the PM or the defence minister to the chief's decision to resign his commission. The heads of the Royal Navy, RN, and the Royal Airforce, RAF decided for now not to follow the former Chief of the Defence Staff instead to remain in their posts for now? The prime minister struck everyone who met him as a very unconventional person, he looked strange compared to other politicians, he changed his appearance when the party had decided to hire a PR, Public Relations, team to help turn the Prime Minister into a more conventional looking politician and not someone who turned up dressed like someone going to attend his allotment. The PM Julien Jones wore ordinary clothes such as bright coloured tank tops and when he wore a suit it was just like one straight off the rack a normal everyday suit and not the more fashionable type of suit he would wear to go with his tank tops ordinary fawn or brown trousers, very much like a 1970's style. He sometimes worn horn rimmed spectacles and he grew a goatee beard. At prime minister's questions time within the house of commons he began to wear suits with smart shirts and a red tie's. At PM's question time he was extremely sharp tongued and quick witted highly intelligent but there was one thing which let him down and it was he seemed to be out of touch with twenty first century politics his own version of politics harked back to political era more suited to the 1970's.

His policies seemed to be from a bygone era more akin to previous decades, the era of union strikes and crippling strikes. He engaged with the younger generation during the lead up to the recent general election. Whereas the previous incumbent in number 10 Downing Street, seemed to have stopped listening to the public and at the people's many fears and as such the previous government ended up taking their eyes off the concerns of the ordinary person much to their cost. For so many in the country during the time the only good thing the previous government were committed to and it was the sorting out the red tape and to successfully negotiate the country's withdrawal from the European Union to free the country from the far-reaching tentacles of the European Parliament. Some of the previous government's MPs certainly became very arrogant towards the voters they started to believe in themselves too much and they knew better than the ordinary person and they eventually ignored the voters much to their cost. Another reason for losing the general election was because of the austerity measures implemented by the previous government. Year on year the then government told the public they would have to tighten their belts even more. After 10 years the voters had enough, and they duly voted the government out of power. But the election vote inadvertently and disastrously let the Marxist leftist government

A Change

of Julien Jones enter power for him to then form a government. He was democratically elected by the many fed up voters around the country the voters wanted a change a new brush. Within weeks of his government of having taking power, they set about making far more and drastic changes they first began by attempting to eradicate the memories and history of what made Britain great. For instance, in and around the palace of Westminster and many of the crown estates so many historic statues were removed and replaced by somewhat modern characters some were statues and busts from other countries, for instance statues such as Churchill, Nelson, Drake Cromwell and Margaret thatcher were removed from public view. Nelsons column and the statue of Nelson himself was removed and the column was re-designated "The Column" eventually Nelson's statue was replaced by a statue of some South American freedom fighter who was plonked on top of a new column having replacing Lord Nelson. The workforce who had been instructed to remove the statues did not agree with the government's decision and so he arranged for the "old historic" statues to the safety of a tunnel in Wales. The tunnels were the same ones that were used to hide many of the works of art from the Nazi's during world war two the tunnels shielded the nation's artwork during the blitz on Britain during the war. The government of the day wanted the workmen to remove all statues and to then melt them down, but the workforce instead had melted lots of scrap metal and produced false destruction certificates to the appropriate governmental department the certificates were proof of destruction of the statues and many of the country's historic works of art. The public were outraged at the destruction of so many iconic statues many people felt there was very little they could do about the government's actions and at the same time the public had no idea of what happened to the statues and it was

14

possibly the best thing, if the government ever found out about the deceit they would have arranged for the statues to be destroyed to their satisfaction. To many it appeared the government were hell bent on destroying the countries cultural heritage and the country's history. The many statues surrounding Whitehall and the houses of parliament were later replaced by statues of African warriors and slaves and of course a statue of the current PM. Support for the Royal British legion, RBL by the latest government soon ceased. The government voted against the RBL's charity status as having deemed and classified it as a political organisation alongside some other notable military charities. The opposition to the government opposed the government's stance but had failed dismally to have the governments ruling over turned. To assist the government stopping many of their policies from being over turned in the future they banned the house of lords from sitting and opposing the governments future policies, the PM used two little used parliamentary acts, they were Acts Nineteen hundred and eleven and 1949. Meanwhile in the house of commons, the government raised a bill to remove many military public statues and monuments dedicated to the various wars Britain had been involved in over many hundreds of years the government wanted the guard's memorial in horse guards to be removed. The other party's MP's within the house of commons were in uproar, they could see the history of Great Britain was being eroded by the current government. No one in the country at the time should have been too shocked because the government laid out their current policies in their party's manifesto which was produced long before the general election. It was a sign of things to come and the opposition party were fully aware of what the newly elected government were capable of. The government owed so many favours to the various unions, the unions backed vocally

A Change

and financially the new government during the run up to the general election and things were about to go from bad to worse. Millions of voters in the country now disagreed with the present government including many of their policies with which they began to implement and many of the voters who had voted for the government during the election now began to feel betrayed only because once in power the government were going back on many of their election pledges and many promises they had made during the run up to the general election. No one in the country seemed to realise just how quickly the government would move to implement many of their latest policies and at the same time they went about authorising the destruction of the very vestiges of history with which made the country what it is today. They made so many promises to the voters and to the various organisations who backed them during the election, it was these organisations with which they could not go back on their promises. The party soon realised one of their major election promises to the many young voters was found to be extremely difficult to implement and it was the abolishment of student university fees. The government surprisingly thought by bringing the nuclear submarine fleet into port they would recover funds needed to keep the fleet at sea and to then use the savings for other needy areas of the country, but they quickly realised it does not work that way. By abolishing student fees there would be a rather large hole in the countries coffers to the extent of roughly a billion pounds.

The PM ordered the treasury to raise the council tax it would mean an average family council tax bill worked out to be @£200 a month, the government changed the rules of council tax and renamed the tax, the tax included the amount of land a property was sat in, such as a large garden. The tax also penalised ordinary people more so than those with large country estates. Within a year there was such bad feeling and growing unrest within the country the anger was aimed directly at the new government. The government were soon looking at raiding The Royal Families privy purse. For George living in his bed sit, in London, life was even more miserable because his council rent, the council tax rose to levels that he could only just afford he found the cost of booze had suddenly shot up all because the treasury raised even more taxes to bring more money into the treasury to fund more of the governments hair brained schemes including its many mad policies, the government were hell bent on nationalise many utilities. George could see things were going to pot, the country had finally been taken over by a Marxist leftist government and it would set about destroying everything which was good about Britain. George was sat in his bed sit dwelling on the past and the comradeship while he served in the Army he still dearly missed the friendship and the comradeship he shared during his military service. He now found that he had far too much time on his hands and he still could not believe the country recently elected a far-left government it made him so frustrated and so angry at the thought of the ordinary people having elected the current government he could not believe just how stupid some people could be. He sat in his flat watching parliament on the BBC, British Broadcast Company, he often observed the PM defending the government's policies. On one of George's trips to his local pub he sat down over in the same corner of the bar where he sat was ideal for the pub's landlady to keep an eye on him as so often George looked extremely aggressive to those who didn't know him. He would normally drink pints of cider but on odd occasions, he would drink a wee dram of whisky. On this occasion the landlady remarked "out celebrating then George or has something special happened"? he was standing at the bar ordering, yet another whisky and replied "no, just this bloody government" with that he then sat back down at his table. She thought to herself "good old George" it wasn't too long before he was once again stood at the bar and ordering yet another pint of cider. The landlady was keeping an eye on him it because it looked as though George was on yet another one of his benders. The local drinkers soon arrived at the pub and one or two of them noticed George was once again sat on his own, someone enquired with the landlady about how long George had been in the pub. By now George was a gibbering wreck, he drank many pints and many glasses of whisky. He paid his bar bill and was by now standing in the middle of the pub where he shouted out, "our time will come, we will overthrow this bloody Marxist government, you lot mark my words" the other drinkers who were standing in the pub shouted in unison "fuck off George you bloody piss head". With that he staggered home from the pub and bounced against a shop window and he somehow managed to head in the direction of his bed sit, call it in built SATNAV. In Russia Ivor was sat in his lonely run down flat drinking from a bottle of vodka he turned on his TV and watched the world news. On one of the TV channels he watched the British PM standing at the despatch box within the houses of parliament The British PM was laying out some new laws to destroy the history of the British people. Ivor may have been Russian, he wasn't happy with his own president he thought his own government were allowing the rich to become even more richer and the poor to become even poorer the President left the Russian people to their own devices and to struggle alone.

There was one thing Ivor liked about the Russian President and it was his President was a very strong leader and wouldn't let any

other nation walk all over Russia without putting up a fight. Ivor
had sympathy for the United Kingdom and its people he often
thought if he could help overthrow the current British
government he would. In America Sam also wasn't happy with
the latest US President. He soon thought the president was off
the wall and he was extremely worried about the direction that
the USA and the President was taking the country. The President
had a novel way of governing the masses including his own
unique method of influencing foreign policy. One of his favourite
methods of communicating was via social media. It did seem to
many whenever the President woke in the morning and it was
perceived the first thing he did was to send messages on social
media seemingly without a care in the world, he did not seem to
care who he may upset through his messages he would send via
text messages. Sam was extremely pissed off with the president.
Many military veterans will easily adapt back into society once
having left the military, but sadly there are some who do not
seem to adapt and who seemingly slip through the gaps and drop
by the wayside no matter hard they try they just don't seem to be
able to adjust. Their experiences and the many memories of their
military service aren't always understood by many of the civilian
population. Their memories of the past also keep many awake
during the night alone fighting their nightmares which stay with
them forever. Life seems to stand still for them, they just can't
seem to move on with their lives!! Too many people who voted
for the latest British government and elected the government
into power seemed to have voted for a massive change in British
politics, there was about to be an earthquake in British politics
not seen for a very long time. The previous government seemed
to bang on at the public to keep tightening their financial belts it
was drummed into the public time and time again, the austerity
policies lasted for over ten years and it was wearing rather thin

with the public, they just wanted a change in government and it was what they got. Consumer prices were sky rocketing at the same time the ordinary persons wages weren't keeping apace, and the ordinary worker was frequently told by the previous PM wages could not rise apart for the politician's wages and the fat cats of industry and the ruling elite. The public could only saw price rises and wages stagnating for many years. The NHS, National Health Service, was in total disarray and the overseas aid budget was grotesquely growing, in the publics eyes, the aid was being wasted and sometimes they heard stories of aid having been sent to countries across the world who hated all what Great Britain stood for. In many people's minds they did exactly what the government and ministers asked of them to do by tightening their financial belts, in the end they could see the NHS collapsing in front of their very eyes and the overseas aid budget continuously being wasted. The government of the day also seemed too many people to be aloof they took their eye off the very people who helped to elect the party into power and subsequently into government. There was a growing mood within the country for a change of government any government would do only if a change was made and very soon. The previous government eventually steered the country out of the EU, European Union. By the time a General Election was called the country had successfully left the Union. Even so the previous government had seriously misjudged the mood of the people. The PM had called an election it had been a few years previously she severely burnt her fingers by once again misjudging the mood of the nation and again she seemingly misjudged the mood of the country. After the country departed from the EU there was no turning back, Europe had its own problems and in Belgium and Spain the provinces also wanted their independence and at the same time Holland also wanted to leave the European Union.

From the Shadows

The former British Prime Minister had thought that the leader of the opposition was a Marxist and left-wing thinker, and, in her mind, she had thought surely the British people would see through him and surely if they had any sense they surely wouldn't vote for his party during the general election. At the same time the sitting governments whose own members of Parliament, MPs, were fighting each other some of the government's own front bench MPs recently voted against the governments legislation and instead voted with the opposition, against their own party's very important policies. It also meant that the opposition leader did not have to do too much all because all he had needed to do was to sit back and let the government of the day shoot itself in the foot and to tear themselves apart, he would be able to step over them and to win the general election. To many people observing the Prime Minister from afar they could see she was her own worst enemy. Her party was tearing itself apart and she did not seem to get a grip on the situation and much to the dismay of her party's supporters. Many ordinary people within the country knew the NHS could not continue the way it was, being mismanaged and so many people were willing the PM to get off from sitting on her hands and to divert some of the countries overseas aid budget to many of the needy institutions, it was the peoples taxes and most people wanted the government to divert some of the money from the overseas aid budget to help save the NHS from an impending disaster, but alas for some reason she and the government did not seem to listen to the publics fears the aid budget was seen as a total waste of tax payers money and in their eyes millions of pounds were wasted. The government continued handing it out to countries who hated western civilisation and the people's way of life. To many people the PM seemed to have become extremely arrogant and the arrogance was at her governments peril. At the

A Change

ballot box the PM and her government were unsurprisingly voted out of power. If the public thought the overseas aid budget was being mismanaged and misspent by the last government, they hadn't seen anything yet? They just had to wait until the Marxist leftist government took over power in government, because they could not wait to get their grubby little hands on the overseas aid budget. George could not believe the "old" party had been ousted at the general election and in his mind the incoming government was the worst kind of government to run any country and he knew the government would eventually run the country into the ground and very quickly. He could still remember when the party was in government back in the 1970's. The memory of the time stuck in his mind it was a very bad time for everyone living in Britain. It would take many decades to recover from the damage inflicted on the country by the then government's actions. In America Sam could not believe the people of the USA elected such a bad president. Week after week the president was either sacking or hiring people into his inner circle within the white house. There was an open sore running throughout his presidency and it was because of a tenuous link to the Russian President. The dark cloud of Russian interference just would not go away. At the same time China was the second richest country in the world only just behind America "the dragon" hadn't yet flexed its newly found wings the country had been hidden away from the glare of publicity all the time building its Navy and its Airforce, at the time its standing Army was the largest in the world it had been for many years, it had been training for a total war scenario. In North Korea's Liaoning province, the largest city is Dandong and very close to the Chinese border. The Chinese weren't so keen to have a war with North and South Korea, it was far too close to its southern border, and of course it could spark a war with America and with North Korea the Chinese would find itself swamped by possibly thousands of North Korean refugees pouring over the Yalu River and into china into the Chines city of Dandong. So, it was much better for china not to be drawn into a war within North Korea it wasn't in its own interest. But there again on the other hand, China was building bases in the south China seas. The world was had changed than let us say ten years previously. Then the world was a much less scary place to live in. Today the middle east and with its melting pot of many conflicts. Iran was hit by many acts of terror within the country many not reported to the western press and kept within the country. Saudi Arabia was fighting a war on its own border with Yemen. Yemen was unable to find peace the Saudi coalition was fighting a proxy war within the country and with such devasting consequences. Britain in the past sold many of the Saudi kingdoms weapons and aircraft. But since the election the newly elected British government showed the world its non-military stance and as such it severed all military supplies and contracts with Saudi Arabia there was a political standoff and the Saudis were seriously considering an oil blockade with Britain. In the United Kingdom many of Britain's defence companies had either gone bust or had reallocated and adapted their businesses to producing non-military products. The PM did not have any sympathy with any of the defence companies and before he became the far-left party leader he previously demonstrated against the arms industry. Now he was the PM he could hurt the British arms industry in the pocket, he thought it was the only language they could understand. With the world in some sort of conflict the many arms companies were making vast amounts of money, out of the utter misery of others. Because of the British governments hostility towards the Arms industry some British Arms companies had decided it was best they move to other countries and to take their business with them, to approach governments who wanted their business and were more than happy to pay subsidies for the British arms companies to set up their factories in their countries. It was a sign of things to come.

Chapter 2 – Politics gets in the Way

The Russian FSB, Federal Security Service, were the successor to the infamous KGB the new organisation learnt very early on and when social media was in its infancy, there was lots of chatter on the internet some of the chatter would provide much information at first much of the information made no sense but as soon as it could be linked to other chatter it would provide a much bigger picture and whenever the information was collated and analysed, the FSB was able to gain much knowledge and build a bigger picture on various Russian citizens and soon became of interest to the security services and those of interest were then added to the states security services databases. Meanwhile the Chinese government also blocked its own citizens from accessing the internet there are so many people in China who are IT, Information Technology savvy and would use the many proxy servers available within the region to access prohibited internet sites. Many of the dissidents in Hong Kong could access much more of the internet than those living in mainland China. The Chinees government were slowly but surely blocking access for users based in Hong Kong. In Russia the FSB created a cyber hacking department and who were accused by the American government of hacking into various American voting databases it was the same voting system used to elect the American President. The FSB cyber department are funded by the Russian military and they view the department as part of the Military's ability to wage cyber war in any region of the world. If a country could somehow access another country's military cyber network then the hackers could in theory access that country's nuclear codes, it would be a proxy war by a cyber hack, no country would ever know who would be next it was a kind of Armageddon via the internet from the comfort of someone sat on a chair on the other side of the world? They could cause mayhem, by just the touch of a button. If they were able active a nuclear first strike without fear of a nuclear retaliation. It all sounds farfetched, but it is not outside the realms of possibility. Russia, China and North Korea were already instigating cyber warfare, not that any country would openly admit to the use of cyber warfare. It didn't mean America, or even the UK did not invest in its capability of carrying out some form cyber first strike warfare, they were keeping their cyber capabilities a very closely guarded secret they wouldn't openly show their hand to the world, it was just like playing a game of poker. Some of the many American IT companies within Silicon Valley were assisting the American military in the art of cyber warfare.

Hence why America were extremely concerned at Britain's choice of Prime Minister and its government. The US President sent a presidential edit to his Armed Forces setting out his instructions to cut immediately any form of cooperation between the two so called close allies, America and Great Britain. The President was most concerned about the possibility of a leak of US intelligence by the UK to undesirable countries. There were also certain people at the top of the UK government who sympathised with known terrorist organisations. To be honest those ministers would never have passed the American government's vetting process and it worried the Americans because they could not afford for their secrets to fall into the wrong hands. The president and his security chiefs were fully aware the British Prime Minister would be privy to high level American intelligence reports that both countries regularly shared hence why the president deemed it necessary to cut back on the Joint Security cooperation between the two countries. Within the British governments election manifesto was a promise to withdraw all together from NATO, the North Atlantic Treaty Organisation. It was yet another decision had worried many of the allies within the organisation. Britain was also a permanent member of the United Nations Security Council. There are four other permanent members. America, China, France and Russia. All five have a vote on world security matters.

The recently elected British government had sympathies towards one or two of the world's rogue states including many terrorist organisations, and with Britain having already withdrawn from other world organisations and important organisations. The British government was building up to having eventually reduced Britain's influence and many commitments across the world. There was one policy the government improved on and it was the overseas development aid budget. After hundreds of years of creating and the building of many of the worlds, worthwhile institutions the country was now withdrawing from many of them and pulling the country's much needed funding. There was one good thing about the government of the day it was the billions of pounds quickly began to be pumped into the NHS, Education and the benefits system. In the end, everything needed somehow to be paid for and it was why when they came into power they were soon "dipping" into the nation's gold reserve and it wasn't a bottomless pit. Another the governments election pledges was not to raise Income Tax. Very soon the treasury soon found Inflation was starting to creep up and the Bank of England raised Interest Rates by two percent it hurt ordinary people in the pocket. The chancellor of the exchequer wanted to wrestle back control of the Bank of England the government's attempts were soon thwarted by "those" in the "city". Many in the financial district of London foresaw what was going on behind the scenes and within government they knew of the track record of all left-wing governments who tried to govern many other countries and who operated in a very similar way. Julien Jones the British Prime Minister studied as a student the various Marxist policies of other left-wing governments. The beginning of things going wrong for the country was when the interest rates in the UK were raised in quick succession, by the government. It hurt those who had a mortgage they soon found paying their mortgages was becoming extremely difficult. The IMF, the International Monetary Fund were extremely concerned about the UK's economy and where it was heading, they sent their findings and its conclusions to the British chancellor of the exchequer the report highlighted the IMF's concerns. As soon as the chancellor reviewed the report he decided to destroy the document with the full knowledge and support of the Prime Minister. Sat in a pub in the Belgium capital Brussels Emile and Bertram were once again discussing how the many bureaucrats within the European Union, EU, had recently voted within the European Parliament for yet more controlling powers over the many individual sovereign states that formed the European Union. For Emile the EU was very much like so many dictators over time and history who had steamrolled over many of the democratically elected governments. The European assembly is an unelected bunch of bureaucrats much like a body of civil servants.

Emile informed Bertram he was contemplating of creating a veterans group on a social media platform, Bertram did not have a clue as to what he meant as he didn't use any social media and he only owned an old typewriter. Emile tried his best to explain to him what he meant but it was all to no avail. They continued to drink and wallow in the good old days of Belgium's great heritage of the past. Bertram was extremely angry at the current spate of terrorist attacks within Belgium. He personally wanted some direct action against those who sympathised towards the terrorists and who were hell bent on killing and maiming so many Innocent people. He believed the EU was dragging its feet regarding the terrorism currently ripping through out the countries of other EU's member states. He may have come across to others as having a biased view on what was happening to Belgium. Emile was not someone who believed in direct aggressive action himself, but because of the many killings he had soon changed his point of view. He wanted to create the social media group to enable like minded veterans to join and to be able to have a good old moan and to reminisce about their own military experiences. Bertram once again warned him against getting too involved in any military veteran's social media group and he warned him the group could possibly be hijacked by for instance a far-right organisation and once again he warned him off from getting involved because he didn't think it was such a good idea, he knew Emile was an adult who could think for himself. They both agreed on the fact the European parliament was such a bad thing for Belgium and it was something they both passionately agreed upon. They were sitting at their favourite place within the pub just as a group of veterans and their friends entered the pub they ordered a round of drinks. The group stayed on in the pub for the duration of the night until it was chucking out time. Emile mentioned to the group about the idea of setting up of a social media group most were up for joining, Bertram was amazed at just how many wanted to be members of a social media site. The rest of the afternoon was taken up with many arguments and differing views regarding Belgium and its loss of influence across the world and how the country's influence was severely diminished and the country's politicians, had in the veteran's eyes effectively handed the country's sovereignty over to the faceless EU bureaucrats housed in central Brussels. Many of the veterans who visited the bar also wanted their government to come down hard on the many supposedly known terrorists who, in their eyes, were living freely within Belgium. The bar staff heard the same group of veteran's moan time and time again, to many of those working in the bar, the veteran's moans were the mutterings of a bygone age the subject matter did not resonate with the staff all because some of them hadn't even been born during the time the veterans served within the military. There was a chap who served in the Belgium Army in West Germany with NATO, North Atlantic Treaty Organisation, He served within the NATAO Headquarters, HQ, at a place in West Germany known as Rheindahlen and the HQ was situated just outside the German city of Monchengladbach. He was stationed there as a Military Advisor during the cold war. He would always reminisce about the many NATO forces bars situated just outside of the "compound" surrounding the headquarters. There was a German, Belgium, Dutch and British bar. Many military service personnel would visit the bars after work on a Friday afternoon and a good time would be had by all, no matter what nation they belonged to. For the members of NATO at the time there was one aim and it was to stop or help to slow down the Soviet forces and the WARSAW pact forces from advancing from Soviet controlled eastern Europe to try to halt them from over running most of western Europe. Parts of West

Germany are perfect tank country, perfect landscape for WARSAW pact and Russian tanks to operate in and to attack at speed to meet their objectives. That was until the iron curtain was eventually pulled down and many of the Eastern European dictatorships were toppled. What was so ironic to Emile including his comrades was the fact Europe seemed to be under a new kind of dictatorship run by the faceless men running the European Union. Before the Belgium veterans left the bar and were still sober many of the veterans agreed to join the new social media group as soon as Emile created it. Once again Bertram warned those sat at the bar of the possible consequences of joining such a group. He was told to shut up and to finish his beer and for now that was the end of the conversation. Meanwhile in St Petersburg Ivor woke from a very restless sleep, he managed to get two hours sleep and the first thing he did was to open a bottle of vodka, it was his normal start to the day. Later, he was due to meet some of his Afghanistan veteran comrades inside their usual bar in St Petersburg on this day was the 38th anniversary of the Soviet Union's invasion of the country. There wasn't going to be any official government celebrations regarding the invasion as it wasn't something the government wanted to celebrate. When Ivor arrived at the bar there was already so many veterans drinking and today there was some veterans who arrived in wheelchairs and some with missing limbs caused by, IED's, Improvised Explosive Devices, sustained during their military service in Afghanistan. The manager of the pub requested the veterans did not make any political speeches or derogatory remarks against the Russian government as he knew he would lose his bar licence if someone reported political speeches being made by any of the veterans. The authorities tried to keep the Afghan veterans quiet. The manager desperately needed the veteran's custom on some occasions, he would turn a blind eye to their political grievances it was a subject that got the veterans going and soon turns into a rowdy brawl. Today, there was to be even more veterans due to arrive at the bar but already there must have been at least fifty or so people and drinking heavily in the bar. After lots of vodka Ivor once again mentioned the possibility of setting up a veterans group on a social media site for many in the bar they were a little unsure because they knew the FSB, Federal Security Service of the Russian Federation would be monitoring the group of veterans online. The Committee for State Security the KGB was disbanded in 1991 and it was taken over by the FSB many in Russia saw no difference in the FSB's method of operations compared to the KGB's ruthless methods. The FSB monitored all social media sites and they were also interested in monitoring the Russian population, they knew knowledge is all powerful. Even though the former Soviet Union no longer existed the current Russian Government were operating its own apparatus to control its citizens and they were nervous of the information freely out there on social media. Many of Ivor's friends within the bar advised him in no uncertain terms not to get involved in social media of any sort if he did he must not to talk about the government to any of the foreigners online. He took onboard his friends concerns he decided to err on the side of caution whenever on the internet. He could not afford find himself on the wrong side of the government and more especially the secret service. He knew he was taking a great risk just being on any social media site.

Over in America Sam woke up from yet another drunken slumber and he had slept off yet another bout of binge drinking, he managed 3 hours of sleep which was good for him. He managed to drag himself to the shower to quickly freshen up, as he felt rotten to the core. He hadn't shaved for almost a week and he now decided to have a shave using the wall mounted mirror in the bathroom and as he began to shave it seemed to Sam that he was shaving away years off his life. After he shaved and finished in the shower and he suddenly looked a totally different person he looked so much younger and felt so much better and he felt almost human. There was one thing he did know, it was that he couldn't do much about his greying and his receding hairline. His daughter and her two children were coming over to his bedsit today with the sole intention of taking him out for a meal. It was the anniversary of Mary, his wife's death. His daughter Sarah knew her father would only have remained sat in his room drinking bourbon to help drown his sorrows and he would wake up the following morning only to repeat the routine of sleeping drinking and sleeping. She took her father to a nice restaurant, no, it wasn't to the local MacDonald's, she knew Sam would often go to have breakfast. Whilst Sam, Sarah and his grandchildren ate their meals he asked the waitress for a double bourbon, it was at this point, Sarah realised her father had desperately needed a drink. During the meal one of Sam's grandchildren Laura mentioned to him about joining a social media site he initially scoffed at the idea of joining social media, but Laura continued to explain about how she had a social media account and told her grandfather about when she was "surfing on the internet" she came across some United States Marine Corps, USMC Vietnam veteran sites. As soon as Laura mentioned the USMC and service in Vietnam Sam's ears seemed to have pricked up and she had her grandfather's full attention. He was very interested in what she said, and he began to interrogate her about the social media sites and what they were all about as he also wanted to know how it worked. Sarah was amused at her father's reaction to what Laura said to him, she hadn't seen her father take so much interest in anything for such a long time and more especially social media. Laura told her granddad "don't worry grandad I will set you up on social media" Sam accepted his granddaughters kind offer and his daughter Sarah laughed "my god dad I don't believe it, don't tell me you are about to join the twenty first century"? Everyone who was sat around the table laughed they were in stiches, Sam didn't know what all the fuss was about. Later in the week Laura came over to her granddads bedsit he owned a laptop and had never used it. His granddaughter opened the laptop she soon created an account with a new password for him and gave it to Sam she connected the laptop onto the shared WIFI they logged onto one of the many social media accounts available and she created an account on one of the military web sites she gave her grandfather the various details to enable him to log onto his new account and onto the military social media account. It was how Sam joined a social media account enabling him to communicate with the wider world. He along with the help of Laura was manoeuvring around the site and he soon contacted a few of his USMC colleagues who also served in Vietnam and at the same time he was serving and fighting deep inside the country. The USMC is a large section of the US Military and it would be very difficult to know who knew who and where they had served unless it could be pinned down to an exact unit or a sub unit. Sam was against the current US government and their ludicrous policies so by joining a social media site he was able to contact some of the other soldiers who served in Vietnam and some of his comrades held similar views about current US politics. Whilst on social media he came across some men who did serve in the same unit as himself and one or two were thinking of setting up a worldwide veteran's social media group for likeminded veterans. Unknown to Sam by having joined the veterans group he was going to be clandestinely monitored by his own governments security apparatus "the land of the free". The scene seemed to be set for many elderly military veterans around the world to share their military experiences on a social media platform.

Chapter 3 - Dissidents

Many of the European military veterans had sometime in their past were all involved one way or another to the eventual defeat of many dictatorships across the world. Some in their service during the cold war having carried out their military service and eventually helping to bring down the Soviet Union's iron grip on Eastern Europe, all of them helped to achieve this feat by having served with NATO during what was referred to as the cold war, Britain was one of the only European country's not to have ever issued a cold war medal to its veterans and it was such a disgrace and was a stain on the nation. Emile was still determined to create the veterans group on social media because in his mind it would help other military veterans to join and to be free to air their grievances and allow them to reminisce about their past military service with likeminded people. His old friend Bertrand was still advising him to err on the side of caution regarding any kind of social media group. As mentioned Bertrand himself didn't use the internet because he didn't trust any of the world's many security services and he knew full well many were monitoring many of the social platform's. In Russia Ivor was once again sat in his favourite bar in St Petersburg the bar was tucked well away from the tourist routes. Once again, he and some of his military colleagues were drinking very strong vodka it was only 09:30 in the morning and it was at this point Ivor once again mentioned the social media site to some of his colleagues and one of his friends Yuri told him in no uncertain terms to stay well away from the yankee media sites because the Federal Security Service, The FSB monitored every known social media site and more, so they concentrate on Russian users. By now Ivor had drunk half a bottle of vodka he didn't give a dam about Yuri's warning. Other members of the group were very reluctant to make a comment inside the bar regarding the social media group they knew there could be members of the dreaded FSB, mixing and monitoring the heavy drinkers within many of the local bars and more especially the bars where it was known military veterans or other dissidents would gather it was the military veterans who were the more vocal in public, possibly due to the amount of vodka they drank. As mentioned previously the FSB were no different to the KGB during the soviet era. Meanwhile in England George was more and more angry at the far-left British government currently in power because in his mind they were attempting to govern the country on a similar style as the old Soviet Union and with similar Marxist values. Inflation was now rampant within the country and George's military pension and war pension were soon eaten into by high inflation and not to mention the money he was paying on his rent, food and various taxes. There were so many disillusioned and disappointed people across the length and breadth of the country, it was soon becoming a country of the haves and the have nots. Many governments across the world did not seem to be very supportive of the ordinary people, who were by now struggling to support themselves. At the same time Britain was the only country in the western world whose people recently and democratically elected a seemingly Marxist far leftist government.

More and more of the country were seemingly being dragged back to how life was in the 1970's and with the many strikes, with the nationalising of many industries and the millions of many people out of work with no future to look forward to. The government recently called a cabinet meeting on the agenda was

37

the oversees aid budget and with a view to divert the overseas aid budget to assist some extremely dubious governments around the world for instances the Palestinian state and of course Cuba. At the meeting there was a very heated discussion regarding sending even more overseas aid to the regime in Syria to help rebuild Syria's infrastructure this was only the start of things to come it was just the tip of an iceberg. The PM also wanted to open Britain's borders to facilitate unconditional access to the country by the thousands of refugees and inadvertently many terrorists would also have unfettered access to the country, the previous government had assisted the then French government regarding the payments from Britain to France to help keep immigrants and the many thousands of refugees within France, but with a Marxist left wing British Government now in power and who's policy it was to have open borders it had meant the refugee problem in France had, all of a sudden and virtually overnight disappeared because Britain suddenly opened its borders to everyone and without any checks?, very much to the delight of the French, the problem had for now also to the relief of the French had now shifted across the channel. George was extremely bitter because he felt the British government was slowly destroying the country and he felt passionately about and he had loyally served. Having a left wing British government in power was in his eyes a dictatorship the government was against every principle he and many others held so dear and believed in and the politicians were soon showing to the people of Britain they were against everything most of the people stood for. He wanted to do something to overthrow the PM including his crony government. He knew he was a minnow taking on a shark. The latest government having been elected soon realised they needed to raise even more finances and, so, they went totally against their election manifesto and began to raise higher taxes across the board and it was yet another reason for George to remain on social media and to participate in spreading the word to hopefully help to bring down the British government. Not that he ever thought he would be able to bring down the government, but he wanted to sow the seeds for its eventual overthrow and because in his mind he was a nobody without any political clout. People power when it can be roused can be an unstoppable force and a force for change? The social media group was eventually setup by Ivor as soon as he set it up, the Russian security services were alerted. Ivor setup the group when he was drunk and as soon as he set it up his account was red flagged by Moscow. The country's military cyber department were alerted immediately and as such they began to monitor Ivor including all those he was in contact with. The FSB could so easily have arrested him there and then, but they didn't as they wanted to see where Ivor would lead them to, possibly to perhaps dissidents who were plotting to topple the Russian state. He could never ever have imagined anyone across the world would want to join the group especially when the administrator was based in Russia? He thought the country shrugged off the KGB apparatus including the spying on its own countrymen way back in the 1990's he naively thought that sort of thing was left in the past, and history, people in the west had to realise any news transmitted in Russia is tightly controlled by the Russian security services and of course the Kremlin. After a week or so Ivor hadn't checked on the social media group as he thought no one would have wanted to join, one morning he decided to just take a peep to see how many veterans had joined the group. He was astounded to see so many veterans joining the site and he could see at first glance see there were hundreds and all with their own stories of their military service. Initially not many veterans from Russia joined the group he could see many vets from around the world decided to join the group. Ivor was ecstatic and very surprised at such a positive response from those living worldwide, of course unknow to him the FSB were monitoring the traffic and more importantly Ivor himself. The Russian state like the Chinese do not allow too much WIFI freedom for its citizens to access the world on the web. In Argentina Lucas found the WIFI a lifeline and a window looking out onto the world. Former enemies had become friends sometimes because of shared experiences and most of all because they also found their own governments cast them aside once they left their countries Armed Forces. On social media a bond was formed and for others in society it could be difficult to understand why so many military veterans had so much in common with each other. Lucas could see the latest veterans of the world group on social media he subsequently applied to join the group and he wasn't the only one to join from Argentina. Many others living in Europe joined and for almost six months all of those who joined were exchanging their "war stories" with each other. Their stories were about their own personal experiences of war and conflicts across the world. Eventually the group soon grew to around two hundred members there were many from such places as America, Canada, UK, Europe, Vietnam and of course Russia. More recently there were members from Australia and New Zealand awaiting confirmation of joining the site. In Brussels Emile once again met with Bertram at their local bar and when he met with Bertrand Emile explained about having joined the veterans group and he went on to explain about a Russian Afghan vet having set up the group suddenly and before he had a chance to explain. Bertrand was horrified at his young friend's decision and he could only envisage trouble with a capital "T". But who the hell was he to tell an adult what to do? Emile seemed happy and very upbeat about having joined the group as his friend's days were normally taken up with drinking himself into oblivion after Bertram's words still ringing in his ears Emile carried on with what he knew was best for him it was spending his days inside the pub drinking. After a few days in London George decided to check on his social media account and on logging on he was prompted online to look at a new worldwide veterans group. When he looked at the group he thought to himself "this looks bloody interesting" once he looked at the subject matter he decided to join the group. Ivor was the administrator and he sent George a message welcoming him on board. Of course, George was someone who's only daily contact with people was at his local pub only if he wanted to talk to others in the pub it was all dependent on the sort of mood he was in.

In America Sam was still in contact with many of his USMC friends many of whom served in Vietnam at the same time as himself. Many of his marine friends were by now living across the world and many of who were trying to escape the nightmare of their service in the Vietnam war. He noticed some of his old comrades were living in Vietnam, the country made such an impact on their lives. He was persuaded by a very good friend to join the new veterans group. Once gain Ivor soon sent him a welcome to the group message, Sam was able to contact so many more of his old comrades. Many months later Lucas was sat in his local bar in the town of San Justo in Argentina as he sat drinking he thought that he would check on his social media account when he noticed one of his "old" comrades from the Falklands war had sent a message regarding the new worldwide comrade's social media group. He checked the group he eventually joined, and just as normal Ivor sent the normal welcome to the group message. Later the same afternoon Lucas felt a lot better about life and he enjoyed his afternoon drinking. Things were seemingly looking up for him. Very soon there were other members of the group who had served in every war and conflict since WWII they all had their own stories and many different experiences having served in the various and many armed forces across the world. On the site there was a chap called Kurt who was from Bielefeld in Germany who had served with NATO in Afghanistan. He was an extremely disillusioned veteran he had become disillusioned with the current German government when he was eventually discharged from the German Army after his national service with the Bundeswehr, German Army, he found himself homeless and hadn't been automatically entitled to a council flat as many ex military before him were, he had to doss down on various friend's sofas for many years until he became entitled to council accommodation.

In France Louis an ex French Foreign Legionnaire soldier also joined the group. He was fanatically anti the current French government and as soon as he was accepted into the group he soon began to voice his opinion regarding the French Government he soon let everyone know what he thought of his own government. So, within the melting pot of the group were many so disillusioned military veterans and they were all griping and moaning about their governments and more so the European Parliament. They were against officialdom and even more so the European Parliament's bureaucracy and the red tape. Not everyone realised at the time users of the social media group were being monitored closely by the Russian security services, FSB, the security operators who were monitoring the group submitted a report to their commanders who then flagged the report for further scrutiny the report eventually reached higher up within the government. A month or so later the monitors were told to keep monitoring the site and to make a note of any further developments. It didn't mean what was noted wasn't important, everything they monitored was of utmost importance to those putting the jig saw pieces together. Meanwhile sat in a modern but a non-descript building within the heart of Moscow was the head of Russia's FSB cyber bureau Sergei who was at the time reading a security briefing pack put together by his internet operators who were monitoring the world wide web 24 hours a day, and within the briefing pack it contained various reports on the many Russian citizens who had recently joined a very popular social media platform and subsequently joined a military veteran's social media group. Sergei noticed Ivor's name kept cropping up time and time again in the report he was acutely aware of his online activities and he was red flagged by the FSB as a person of great interest to the security services. Because of his interest to the FSB he was totally unaware of his interest to any of the Russian security services.   The head of the cyber bureau read the file and as soon as he finished reading it he sent its contents together with his own conclusions to a higher level within the department. A day later Sergei received a priority message from a someone much higher up within higher command all the message said, was just two words "continue monitoring" it was a short and very much to the point. The monitoring team had by now had created a database of the other members of the group included were those living across the world. The list made for an interesting read, for instance George was on the list it also included Sam and Emile. It was exactly what Emile's friend Bertram had predicted and it was the sort of thing would eventually happen. Meanwhile in Moscow Sergei ensured each Friday his team of monitors submitted a report to him and it included every member of the veterans group including their chat, each month he would send a condensed report to the head of the FSB's cyber directorate. So far Ivor was left to his own devices by the Russian security forces, for the FSB at the same time were more interested with the foreign members of the group only because some of the members might be of some value to the FSB in the future. After six months of monitoring the head of the directorate requested as much data that could be gathered on the Belgium member called "Emile" soon the cyber security team put together a "personal biography" on Emile. The directorate wanted to know where his loyalties lay? could they use him in their plans to undermine Europe. They needed to find out who his friends are including his enemies. There was already some Russian "agents" serving in Brussels and the FSB team in Belgium soon found out where he drank and where he lived in the city much of the data was on the social media site, it wasn't too difficult to track him down. Each day he had the same routine he would visit the same bar to have the "odd" beer the agent shadowing Emile sat inside the same bar as Emile to enable him to observe and the old man Bertrand and of course their veteran friends. One afternoon the group were very loud and raucous. The FSB agent Alexei enquired with one of the barmaids about. He asked if it was someone's birthday party one of the barmaid's replied it's the "old" man's birthday some of his old military colleagues were celebrating with him she said, "mind you they don't need an excuse to get pissed". Alexie needed to identify Emile and to somehow obtain a photograph of him and without blowing his cover or to make the group suspicious of what he was up to. He asked the barmaid to point out who was who in the group, unknown to her he switched on the Dictaphone, on his mobile phone and as she helpfully pointed out who was who within the group, she had to admit that she didn't know everyone sat at the table with Bertrand. She identified Emile, Alexei still needed to try and get a picture or at least a picture of the group. Members of the group began to take pictures with their mobile phones including the waitress, she wanted some photographs to display within the bar area. Alexie gave the waitress his mobile she didn't mind as everyone else in the bar were drunk and didn't raise any objections, once again she approached the group and began to take pictures and hadn't raised any suspicions. An hour or so later the group began to sing rousing military songs and it was soon time for Alexie to leave the bar his task completed, and it was carried out with some relative ease and luckily, he hadn't been compromised, he quickly blended into the shadows from where he came from and left the bar. At the FSB office in central Brussels he handed his mobile phone to the IT whizz kid he soon downloaded the photographs from the mobile he used some very smart piece of software to enhance the pictures. As soon as the whizz kid finished working his "magic" he contacted Alexie for him to come and take a look at the pictures and to identify Emile, he arrived at the IT operators office and took a look at the photographs and pointed out Emile, the technician cropped him out from the main group of people in the bar he enhanced the photographs even more Alexie said, "perfect my friend" now could you please download all the pictures onto this memory stick and once the download was completed he took the stick to his office. He put together his report into what he managed to gather at the bar and he reported on what he found out and he also identified Emile in the pictures. He sent the files to the FSB headquarters in Moscow, the files were sent via a secure encrypted means. After he sent the files he could relax a little and he opened a small bottle of Russian vodka. He always thought his time in Belgium would be interesting and right now it was beginning to get interesting he began to feel that his time in Belgium was worthwhile. He was not privy to those running the

FSB far away in Moscow. Back in London George was becoming more disillusioned with the British government. The FSB looked and analysed George's social media outpourings, but the head of the Russian security apparatus wasn't interested in George per say. As the current left wing British government were good "friends" with Russia they were friends for many years besides the government were doing everything the Russian government had wished them to do without needing to apply any pressure. At that precise moment in time the Russians only wanted the British Government to do was to destroy the countries, nuclear weapons. Russia's foreign policy was to disrupt all western governments from within, as at that moment in time they could not be seen to be getting their hands dirty or caught red handed getting involved with the downfall of democratically elected government. It was a delicate balance and juggling act, but in Britain's case it was doing such a great job all on its own. One of their major aims was to topple the American government. The FSB invested a great deal of resources into the "American affair". The problem with the President of the USA had become unconventional and inconsistent regarding worldwide foreign policy. There were a few nations who were surreptitiously trying to influence or attempting to create false news within America. The American government systems were designed for such a situation there were so many failsafe procedures in place to protect the American people and its institutions from such a scenario. The FSB had their own procedures to try to surreptitiously undermine any US government. All the Russians needed was an ideal opportunity to put their plans in action.

Meanwhile George had recently posted some extremely strong worded feelings regarding the British government he aired his views on social media and after a heavy drinking session. The British monitoring organisation GCHQ, The Government Communications Headquarters was monitoring George for a few weeks he was now flagged as a person of interest but only as a low-level risk. George became even more disillusioned regarding the current state of the country he was never satisfied about much the government was doing or what they were telling the public, no change there then? In Brussels Emile was once against sat in his local bar with Bertram and some old friends. They were ripping apart the youth of today Bertram jumped on the bandwagon he was slagging off the youth of today he mentioned that some had no backbone and were good for nothing, forgetting everyone one sat at the bar were youngsters themselves and not in the too distant past and at the time there would have been similar people knocking them at the same age. The same barmaid was working in the bar she was the same one who was working when Alexie recently asked her to take some photographs of the group celebrating Bertram's birthday. What she was totally unaware of was the man asking her to take the pictures and who was talking to her was in fact recording everything she said by using the Dictaphone on his mobile phone. This morning Emile had been drinking at home he polished off half a bottle of wine, when he arrived at the bar he was very loud, argumentative and a little drunk. Bertrand was extremely concerned about his younger friend. It was by now 11:30 am and the group had been joined by two other veterans. Recently there had been a bombing outrage at one of the Brussels underground Railway stations of course it was the main subject of the groups conversations. Emile announced to those gathered "give me a bloody pistol and I will take out the scumbags one by one I have nothing to lose, comrades who is with me"? His old friend was very alarmed at his outburst he was also very concerned at his friends change of mood. He told him he was a bloody fool to announce such a thing in a public place. He went on to say it had been a dangerous thing to say in times like these. Others sat around the bar berated Bertrand for his remarks they saw it as an affront to their own views. For them Emile only said what they were all thinking, they just didn't have the balls to air their views in public as he had. After the group left the bar Emile arrived home and logged onto his social media account once again continued to air his views to the world via social media. He mentioned what he said earlier in the bar. A few veterans in America including Sam agreed with his outpourings via the internet. In London George also read Emile's outpourings with great interest. But he hadn't remarked on the post as he remained silent he did agree with some of the points raised. Deep down George wanted to topple his own government, he just didn't know how he could legally and legitimately carry out such an undertaking. The seeds of disillusionment were sown throughout the internet. His resentment was aimed at the younger generation it was deep seated as he believed it was the younger generation who voted and subsequently helped to elect the so called "Marxist" government into power. The nation's security forces were extremely worried the government were going to seriously cut the military budget. The head of the armed forces wanted to prove to the new government the military were in fact indispensable and were needed to fight terrorism and British interests across the world. There were many in the government who wanted to disband more of the security apparatus. There was another problem facing the security services the government were going to enforce an "open doors" policy at the country's borders in other words the border checks were coming down. There was potential for conflict between the various government departments. The head of MI5 was aware of the government's policy regarding the military and the various security agencies and it was recently highlighted by their decision to place the nation's nuclear submarine fleet in dock. There were issues between America and the United Kingdom over sharing intelligence it was because of the UK's stance on the nuclear issue and its lack of security measures. The new "friends" it was talking to caused America to re-think the sharing of highly classified security information between the two nations. Because of the latest British government's policies there was soon a run on the pound and inflation was rife. The chancellor was dipping into the countries gold reserve, the countries nest egg. He was selling gold to help fund some of the governments brainless policies, the problem was the gold reserve would soon be gone and at the rate it was being spent there would be nothing left for a rainy day.

The government was talking about raising taxes on almost all goods and services they were looking at raising VAT, Value added tax. Meanwhile George was spending many hours on line and in contact with his new found, friends. He had a lot to say about how the British government were systematically destroying the country that he passionately loved and held dear. In Belgium Emile contacted George and he expressed his own opinion on the current British government and he sympathised with him. In Moscow the FSB cyber department noticed the extra traffic between him and George the FSB operators thought George was an interesting character and was worth flagging up for further investigation and monitoring. One of the monitoring operators typed up a short report all about George she sent it to Sergei. He noted the report and asked for George to be red flagged. As far as the Russian government were concerned the current UK government were doing exactly what the Russian President wanted there was no need to further undermine the government of the day as they were doing alright on their own. The Russians were hoping to find a way of finding a contact in Belgium to possibly influence the European Headquarters by fair means or foul. It is where Emile could play an important role in their plans, everyone has some worth in the world of espionage and as soon as they fulfil their usefulness they can be thrown to the wolves. The FSB by now were showing a great deal of interest in the new veteran's social media group the dossier they were holding on some of the members was by now steadily growing. At the same time George over in London wasn't of any interest to those in Moscow Britain's government was doing an excellent job of destroying the country's defence capabilities all on their own and so Moscow decided to leave George alone, for now that was. The Americans despaired at the state of the UK and its government as they slowly began to withdraw from the various joint institutions and from funding them. American funding was by now reduced to a trickle and it would not be too long before it ceased. The British chancellor of the exchequer once again dipped into the countries gold reserve to help pay for some of the governments hair brained election pledges. Taxes had been raised including and more from income tax. In London George became more despondent with the government. Everyone at some time has a right to moan at their own government but the current British government were beginning to turn the country into a "banana republic". The Marxist leftist prime minister was formulating agreements with the "old" style Marxists governments across the world and diverted overseas aid to similar governments who were suppressing their own people, within the British public there was mutterings and growing dissent regarding how the country was currently being run. In Germany the government disastrously failed to gain a working majority within the Reichstag, the German parliament. The chancellor of Germany her power was seriously reduced, the government had needed to urgently form a coalition if not, they would be forced into calling for a general election. Kurt voted against the current government, as he could never forgive the chancellor for having an open-door policy for refugees because and he thought the country would not be able to assimilate so many people in one go and to expect them to assimilate into German society. He vented his anger on social media he expressed extreme right-wing views. Even Ivor the social media group's administrator felt he needed to warn Kurt to tone down his thoughts and to refrain from airing his far right-wing views online. In America Sam was someone else who was very disillusioned with the latest incumbent in the White House who seemed to divide and conquer via twitter he was sacking members of his staff on a regular basis; the country was split about what was happening in the country. Sam was grateful for the Walton care, medical cover, he finally qualified for the free medical care. But as soon as the current president was elected one of his major policies was to evoke the Walton care altogether Sam was extremely worried at the change of policy because he did not have private medical care. He once again took to social media to vent his anger. As the FSB continued to monitor the social media site they soon realised the majority who joined the site were disgruntled ex-servicemen who held a grudge against their own governments and they had their own individual reasons for being so angry. The FSB were still maintained a database on everyone within the group, they were very thorough. The reason behind keeping such a list because at some point someone on the list may at some point will be very useful to the FSB, they were in it for the long haul and were experts on collecting data for future assignments. George was sat as usual in his local pub quietly reading the morning newspaper. The landlord kept a very close eye on him as he would never know which George would turn up? The good George or the pain in the arse George because no one could tell. Meanwhile the UK government was trying hard to get through parliament new legislation to convert major private companies such as British Gas, the Railways, the electricity industries and British Telecom, BT, back to state owned and state run. The outlay to carry it out would be billions of pounds somehow the government would have to find the money from somewhere, more taxes perhaps? It was a promise made by the government whilst in opposition to the unions. For many in the country it was uncertain times.

The government was trying to rollback, decades of business and turn the country back to the nineteen seventies. George knew everyday costs would soon rise and his own taxes would increase to help pay for the governments outlandish ideas and policies. Those in the country who were worth vast amounts of money would always invest in the governments projects and as such would make even more money and become even more wealthy off the back of others who were by now finding it very difficult just to get by. At the same time the opposition party was a minority in parliament and could not block the governments legislation or their policies it meant almost all the government's policies would have to get through a vote in parliament. George felt he needed to do something and to somehow bring the government down he eventually came up with an outlandish idea to bring the government to its knees, it wasn't via the ballet box for him his aspirations were only a pipe dream. Meanwhile in Russia Ivor became more and more outspoken regarding the Russian President. He was spouting off about how he thought the president should gather up his ill-gotten gain and retire or even leave the country and to let real democracy spread its wings across the country. He felt just like most citizens living in Russia the country wasn't democratic since the downfall of the old communist way of governing he like most thought all that happened was one dictatorship was being replaced by a much subtler one the President was just like a modern-day tsar. In America Sam was very despondent with what was happening with the latest president. In Belgium Emile hated the way his government had succumbed, without a fight, to the European council. Everything the Russians were monitoring on the veteran's social media site pleased them as they knew they could so easily manipulate someone within the group for their own political ends. Sergei was very close to recommending to Moscow a new plan of action. The FSB wanted to create a massive impact on the world stage and they wanted something to hit the world headlines without being traced to a Russian plot they couldn't be seen to have blood on their hands. In Argentina Lucas was becoming confused about himself, he felt this way since returning to Argentina at the end of the "Malvinas War", "The Falklands War" he soon became a nobody and began to feel like he was invisible to the rest of society, a common feeling for lots of military veterans across the world. In Moscow it was soon time to decide in what direction the FSB were planning to move. It was soon time to implement a plan of action. At the same time the Russian President was undecided, and he was worried about the actions of the Russian state might carry out could so easily, be traced back to the Kremlin or even the FSB, so any plans were put on hold, for now. Unknown to many people living in Russia the President had been formulating a "master plan" his mind it would be a more daring plan of action and one which would be deliberately traced to the Russian Government.

Dissidents

Chapter 4 – Hesitant

The Russian's were more than happy with Britain's antics because the British Government were playing right into the Russian's hands. All because of the UK's withdrawal from many of the world's worthy and more valued institutions. One of the most important decision having been taken by the British was the country's withdrawal from NATO and the UN. Russia was waiting on the side lines for the domino effect to begin and for the eventual collapse of the NATO alliance. At the same time America had every reason to be alarmed at the goings on in the UK and of course Europe. America was there to help and to "bail out" Europe. During the two world wars the US had shed the blood of so many of its citizens in helping to bail out Europe and to help throw off the yoke of the Nazi occupation of most of Europe. The president was extremely reluctant to bail out Europe in another war on his own and he wanted the UK to "do its fair share" on the world stage if the British government were reluctant to do so, then he wasn't prepared to "help" Americas closest ally any more. The Russians had a plan to surreptitiously speed things up in Europe to help start the domino effect. The Russian president called for a security debate in the Russian parliament, the state duma, where he addressed the assembly regarding the perceived threat to the Russian western border by NATO forces. The Russian president wanted a vote for him to have even more control of Russia's armed forces and for a much larger arms budget to help purchase the latest in military equipment, it went without question both of his requirements were voted in the favour of the president. At the same time around the world there was so much information on social media, also in the press and TV misinformation was generated by those in power it was used for their own aims, in some instances it was used to surprisingly mislead their own people. The Russian president summoned the head of the FSB to his office within the Kremlin. During the same time the UK's government was in direct contact with the pentagon through the channels the allies had open to them and the UK government informed the US Military to the fact Britain was soon closing all the United States bases within the United Kingdom. The US Défense Secretary could not believe what he was being told he was incredulous and that was putting it mildly. He immediately informed the President who demanded to see the document the British Ministry of Defence sent to the pentagon he needed to see the document to believe what he was being told, it was a potential diplomatic incident and could so easily lead to the severing of all US/UK links. He sat in the oval office his personal secretary printed the document sent by the pentagon he placed the sensitive document on the president's desk. The president had to read the document twice over and after he had assimilated the details contained in the letter he then picked up his telephone and demanded to be put through to the British Prime Minister in London. There hadn't been the normal peasantries when he was eventually put through to No 10 downing street in London and his first words were "Prime Minister I have just received a communique from your Ministry of Defence informing me of your governments wish to close all of the US military bases in the United Kingdom, now tell me it is a load of crap" the PM lamely replied, "yes it is correct the and UK is going to become a Nuclear free country a neutral country in any time of war and therefore my government respectfully request your military forces to leave the UK". The President responded, "bull shit" he slammed the phone down on the PM, Julien Jones. As the president sat in his chair thousands of miles away he shouted, "what the fuck has just happened here" he called for every senate member and the defence chiefs to a meeting at the Whitehouse for the following day as it was deemed very important and no one was to be excused. He was fuming and some in his office could have sworn they could see steam escaping from the president's ears. Of course, the ordinary person living in both countries did not have a clue to what was going on behind the scenes. In the UK the latest opposition party could have so easily have predicted what was happening to the country now it was being run under a Marxist government, never to the degree it recently escalated to and in such a short period of time. Meanwhile the Chinese Navy intercepted some radio traffic emitting from a US re-supply vessel, it was the supply vessel for an Americans Virginia class Nuclear submarine. The vessel was in the China Seas the ship mistakenly transmitted an un coded message ordering the ship to meet up with its host a US nuclear submarine had already changed course for the North Atlantic. The Chinese Navy picked up the transmission and was given permission by the Chinese government to relay the message to the Russians, who naturally found the information most interesting to say the least. It was most unusual for the submarine to move from the China seas to the North Atlantic the information supplied by the Chinese to the Russians had allowed them to plot the submarines course to roughly work out how quickly the submarine could travel and enter the North Atlantic and they could place one of their hunter submarines in the North Atlantic along with its support vessel. It was all due to the United Kingdom withdrawing their nuclear submarine fleet back to their respective home ports and so currently there wasn't a single British Nuclear submarine patrolling the North Atlantic hence why the Americans needed to withdraw one of their submarines from the China Seas it was because there now wasn't any nuclear deterrent in the North Atlantic or the Norwegian sea it would mean that any Russian Nuclear submarine could now be able slip out from their Russian submarine base in or around Murmansk the Canadians had also monitored an increased movement of Russian non nuclear vessels and much more naval activity in the Atlantic and accordingly they informed the Americans. The added concern was the Russians would be able probe how far the UK would go to intercept Russian aircraft or naval vessels. Soon Russian bombers were probing British airspace and the RAF, Royal Air Force, were informed by the secretary of state for defence to cease the interception of any Russian aircraft. On one occasion two Russian long-range bombers flew over central London and some elderly people watched the bombers fly over the city they hadn't seen any "hostile" military aircraft fly over the city since they were children and during the second world war. The aircraft made such a sight flying so high in the sky to many watching the aircraft flying over Buckingham Palace to be able to fly so deep into British airspace was unheard of. On the tail of the aircraft was the Russian flag and a red star. An elderly lady standing in the crowd and who as a child personally witnessed German bombers flying over the London docks she never thought that she would ever again witness a foreign aircraft flying again over London and it made for an eerie sight. Someone in the crowd shouted, "where are the bloody RAF, Royal Air Force"? The two aircraft were eventually intercepted by an RAF Typhoon Eurofighter. The typhoon was not there to aggressively intercept the bombers it was there to escort the Russian aircraft. It eventually escorted the bombers to RAF Brize Norton an RAF airfield in Oxfordshire it was because the base had a landing strip large enough to accommodate the two bombers. For Russia sending the bombers to probe British airspace had proved to them how placid and neutral the UK military and government had become in such a short space of time. The Russian President was by now assured and he was extremely confident that he could afford to move resources to other areas of the world all because of the UK's lack of aggression and its inability to defend itself from an aggressive enemy. After the bomber incident the United States Military based in the pentagon were seriously concerned some of the military were very angry at the British government's lack of response to the Russian incursion into British airspace.

It didn't look so good!!

Across the world all the news channels showed film footage of the Russian bombers flying across London in broad daylight. In almost every country it was breaking news. The Russians were in seventh heaven it was such a great coup and by now the Russian bombers and the air crews were by now back home in Russia the crews were being hailed as hero's. George was sat in his flat cursing the British government, more so the head of the armed forces he knew it was only the beginning of things to come. He decided to visit his local watering hole. He saw enough of the news for one day he was fully ashamed at the governments lack of response. In America the news coverage of the events in London was stinging and it was aimed solely at the British government's lack of response to the Russian aircraft entering British airspace without any response, it would never have happened in America.

Meanwhile in London the PM and the cabinet along with the secretary of Defence were putting the final touches to a draft bill for the Prime Minister to put before the house of commons it set out to reduce the border agency to allow even more free movement of immigrants and refugees to freely flow into the United Kingdom and without a single check by customs or the border organisation. Some ministers within the cabinet were totally against the PMs proposal but had been overruled by the party's chief whip. It was all due to the government having a ruling majority at the house of commons and the opposition were weakened and powerless to vote down the governments bill or any other of the government's proposals that were put forward to the house of parliament. The shadow home secretary was astonished at the government's proposal to do away with all immigration and all border restrictions it was an open-door policy for any terrorist wanting to wreak havoc in the country. Many British fighters soon began to trickle back from fighting in the middle east and from fighting in North Africa and they were by now unhindered from entering the country for them to inflict terrorist atrocities within the UK. The PM was taking a great interest in the countries overseas aid budget, he took over the legacy from the previous government of providing 0.7% of the country's Gross National Income on the overseas development aid each year. When his party were elected into government the overseas aid budget was at £15 billion and it was a substantial amount of money more especially when ordinary people were desperately trying to make ends meet. The incoming government had many affiliations with Marxist and terrorist organisations across the world. The PM wanted much of the overseas aid to be switched to help fund some of the organisations many of whom despised Britain and what the country stood for, but they were more than happy to accept the county's generous aid. America was extremely worried about Britain and the so called "special relationship" between both nations. At the same time the British government would have to work out a method of safely destroying the country's Nuclear arsenal. The PM was even considering approaching the Russians for assistance in destroying the nuclear submarines and if they did it would be music to the Russians ears. There were one or two high ranking British military men who eventually got wind of the PM's draft proposal and duly tipped off the Americans, the Americans could not act on the information alone more especially when it was from unconfirmed sources. The Americans were by now forewarned and devising a plan of action to stop the UK's nuclear weapons ever falling into Russian hands, it included various daring military options, some could have been considered an act of war? The American president did not possess a sense of diplomacy he seemed to be conducting his own and unique form of diplomacy via social media. He was very close to talking his nation to war via social media. The world of diplomacy had been turned on its head all because of a small group of world leaders, one being the most powerful world leader. The world was a very different and a far more dangerous place to live in than say only a year prior.

A month later China had deployed one of its latest warships a type 54A frigates into the Mediterranean Sea and it wasn't the first time. the frigate was escorted by a supply ship providing it with fuel and provisions. The warship and supply ship soon docked at Algiers in Algeria to take on board fresh supplies and much needed fuel. The ships soon set sail in the direction of the Atlantic Ocean but both Chinese warships ships were being monitored by the Royal Navy in Gibraltar also by Spain and France including Portugal's tiny navy. The Royal Navy based in Gibraltar were informed by the Ministry of Defence in London to remain in port and remain there until further notification. The military in Gibraltar were astounded by the reply and so it was left to the Navies of Spain, Portugal and France to "shadow" the Chinese vessels. There hadn't been any exchange of intelligence with Britain. The other nations Navies had continued to shadow the Chinese vessels and without any assistance from Britain. Britain was by now blind regarding to where the Chinese vessels were heading, and it was only satellite technology and listening to the Chinese radio traffic which gave some clues to the British military intelligence service. The Joint Headquarters in London soon learnt some of the American satellites were currently inaccessible to the British, whereas the Americans in the past would allow the British military to have full and unhindered access to the American Satellites including military intelligence data. Also, by now many of the US military liaison men and women were withdrawn from many of the British Military headquarters and the British military were denied free access to all US military intelligence and their satellites passwords and code used by the MOD had been deleted. The two Chinese warships were by now tracked passing the Bay of Biscay skirting the Atlantic Ocean onwards past Brittany, just off the North west coast of France the Chinese naval ships soon entered the English Channel once again the British government kept the Royal Navy warships tied up in port all RAF attack aircraft were kept on the ground and in their hangers. The French government was astounded at the lack of British military action including the total lack of cooperation the French president personally contacted the British Prime Minister and informed him in no uncertain terms, of the French nations concern at Britain's distinct lack of response to both the Russian military aircraft crossing into British airspace and of course the latest incident regarding the lack of cooperation or the distinct lack of action by the United

Kingdom whatsoever regarding the two Chinese naval vessels accessing international waters including the English channel. He came off the telephone knowing full well the British prime minister was a pacifist and he was showing his true colours. The PM had put the fear of god into the French president because in his eyes the British government had just sat on its hands regarding the Chinese warships incursion in and around the west section of European seas and the lack of any action or assistance by the RN and RAF. It began to sink into the French President's mind, that only a few miles off the coast of France was a country ripe for the picking it could so easily end up being a jumping off point for terrorists or a pariah state to attack the region without a military response from the British government. He had a gut feeling Britain would roll over and capitulate. Or the French could have a neighbouring country just a few miles across the channel who could be involved in a civil war, it was not such a farfetched conclusion. The French and Spanish governments were incensed at Britain's lack of cooperation while escorting and monitoring of the Chinese vessels inside European waters. The French and Spanish Ambassadors in London had delivered a very strongly worded communique to No 10 Downing street. It was a highly unusual approach and it showed how the countries fellow allies were disgusted at the lack of British cooperation and showed the British governments true hand regarding the response in international events. The news of the Chinese incursion into the English Channel was all over the press and with the recent Russian incursion into British airspace it was extremely worrying. In his local pub George was sat reading the newspapers and he was angry at the current state the country found itself in. There were murmurings in the UK of a foreign country exerting its influence during the last UK general election and it was only hearsay, nothing more than that as such there wasn't any hard proof of any wrong doing by any outside agencies it was well known the Russian's recently spent billions on building its cyber warfare capability. Besides if it could be proved let's say if it was the Russians, it didn't make any sense because they were more than confident in the UK's government and its own ability to reduce Britain to a miss managed country and ran like a banana republic sat close to mainland Europe.

The Russians could not have made a better job of bringing a country to its knees even if they had tried. Their aim was to topple NATO and the European union by any means fair or foul. Both NATO and the European union was spreading their influence far too close to Russia's borders and if NATO wanted to antagonise the Russians they were doing a very good job of it. In the Baltic states NATO was stationing more and more troops and military hardware too close to Russia's borders and neighbouring countries. Russia was fast becoming extremely alarmed at NATO's true intentions. The EU was pouring billions of euros into some of the former soviet union's areas of interest and some areas they themselves occupied during the cold war just as Europe was spreading its influence, into eastern Europe, albeit with the help of the Euro. At the NATO headquarters in Brussels, Belgium, the NATO secretary general called for a meeting of all 29 member, states. The secretary general was so concerned about Britain's seemingly lack commitment to NATO and the alliances core values. The secretary general was moved to call on all 29 members to attend the meeting because three countries recently complained at the highest level regarding Britain's total lack of cooperation during the so called "Chinese" incident and the USA felt it was an affront for a country like Britain to reduce its military capability to such a level. For Britain to expect other countries to provide military protection to the country, it wasn't going to happen because it is not how the world works.

The USA had submitted a motion regarding Britain's decision to withdraw its nuclear submarine deterrent and its ludicrous decision to bring its fleet back home to their submarine bases. Meaning a large chunk of NATO's nuclear capability was severely reduced. Because of Americas complaint the meeting was upgraded to a formal NATO summit it would also mean each one of the heads of states would need to attend. It was one summit the British PM would be wise to attend and in person. The USA was going to raise the issue of reducing Britain's diminishing influence both in the UN and within NATO. The Americans wanted to take Britain's permanent seat away in both alliances. It would be a serious move by NATO and possibly the UN. The British point of view wasn't strong the government was still hell bent on reducing its nuclear deterrence and its military strength. It also wanted to reduce its commitments to the UN and to NATO. Britain was seen verging on having the smallest army in Europe. The Royal Navy was non-existent, and its naval ships were kept at various naval docks. The Royal Airforce was very low on highly trained pilots all due to the lack of flying hours. The government passed a recent motion reducing the government's commitment to the Armed Forces of at least 2 % of GDP, gross domestic product. In the first year in power the government had managed to reduce it to 1.5%. The heads of the military were up in arms at the government's recent decision. Some threatened to resign, the Minister for Defence and the prime minister responded by letting the heads of the military leave the pair would not stop them from choosing whatever they wanted to do, in other words they called their bluff. What was happening in the

Hesitant

United Kingdom was NATO's worse nightmare over the many years the country was one of the organisations staunchest allies, but the current UK government was putting the countries defence at risk. NATO had planned for many scenarios but not for the one which was currently playing out in the UK. On social media the chatter was about Britain's apparent pacification and George was the first person to vent his anger over the social media platform. In Belgium Emile was astounded at the UK government's current stance and its apparent passive agenda. More so, because the world was now a turbulent and un predictable place to live in than a year previously. The various members of NATO were starting to think that they could no longer rely on Britain to honour its commitments to the alliance the country had now weakened the remaining member states, from any outside aggression towards them. Part of the summit would be for each head of state to renew their countries commitment to NATO. It was the only way the secretary general more especially the president of the United States would know if the British government were committed to the alliance to also see if the government were bluffing about their threat to withdraw from the alliance.

In Moscow the FSB had been putting together a master plan that would affect the world and more directly those living in Europe. They would have to wait first for the outcome of the upcoming NATO summit. The FSB had so many agents and sympathisers within NATO and the European parliament and they would get to know about the NATO summits outcome very quickly. On social media Kurt in Germany became active and very angry he hadn't been online for a few months and was disgusted at the way the UK government was going about its business. This got George going and he was once again on his high horse and he agreed with everything Kurt posted on social media. The FSB were still monitoring the site and Serge was sending monthly reports to his masters within the FSB headquarters. The US president recently tweeted about what he thought about the situation in Britain under the current government. The Prime Minister obviously read the tweet he immediately sent a communique to the British ambassador in Washington he wanted his message to be hand delivered personally to the American president, accordingly the ambassador was granted an audience with the president and inside the historic oval office. The president stood up from his desk to shake the hand of the ambassador. What surprised the ambassador was the famous bust of Churchill was moved from its normal place and placed on the president's desk. The president noticed the ambassador was looking at the bust, it was part of his plan he invited the ambassador to sit down. The moving of the bust was just a ploy to show respect to the people of Great Britain, but there was no respect towards the current British government. The ambassador handed the Prime Ministers communique to the president and he opened the envelope he started to read its contents as soon as he read the letter he immediately ripped up the letter into small pieces. He then spoke to the shocked ambassador "bull shit" and politely invited the British ambassador to leave the oval office. Once the ambassador was back in his office within the British Embassy he conveyed to the prime minister the presidents reply as soon as it was conveyed to the PM he put the phone down and cut off the ambassador. Diplomacy between the two countries was by now at an all time low. For some people within the Whitehouse had thought the president was extremely refrained during the meeting with the British Ambassador. The prime minister's communique was very timid, to say the least, all it conveyed was

Hesitant

"Her Majesty's British Government is extremely disappointed at the president's recent tweet the Prime Minister asked him to refrain from making future political statements between the two countries more specifically aimed towards the British government because the President was undermining the good work the British government was carrying out across the world" hence the Presidents remark "bull shit". He hadn't deemed it necessary to send a reply. America was by now viewing Britain as a Marxist government. Meanwhile the country was switching its overseas aid budget to more and more bizarre leftist and dare say to some terrorist affiliated organisations who were based in the middle east. The chancellor of the exchequer was driving more and more businesses from the UK to mainland Europe because he was taxing companies heavily and unfairly. He and his department, the treasury department, were making a pig's ear of the country's finances. It would take future generations many years to sort out the financial mess unless the country could find masses of oil be it from the North Sea or from shale fracking? It was in the future and it was the here and now which was more worrying. Most of the financial houses including the banks were heavily taxed as always and the additional costs were passed onto the consumer. When the government was in opposition they had voted against the proposed anti terrorism legislation but now they were in power the prime minister wanted to deploy troops to war when there was a clear mandate and a need to do so. That was if the government hadn't decimated the Army by then. He was still putting together the governments latest resolution to turn Great Britain into a neutral state because it was his governments long-term goal at the same time he thought the war on terror was not working and didn't yet have a solution. It was of his own making and he just couldn't rectify the situation the country found itself in. There was talk of Britain pulling much of its military force from the Falkland Islands and much to the glee of the Argentinian government, and to the condemnation of the Falklands Legislative Assembly. The British governments thinking, was because of the Falkland Islands situated thousands of miles away from Britain they are closer to South America than to Britain, in the mind of the British Prime minister the Falklands War was a thing of the past the Islands were draining money away from the British tax payer. The PM did not want to seem antagonistic towards Argentina and so his secretary of state for Defence and the MOD, Ministry of Defence, was tasked to come up with a Strategic Defence review of the British forces on the Islands with a mind to reducing the British military garrison, it was perceived by many in government there wouldn't be a need for a large military force after the country had withdrawn from NATO. The Argentinian government could not believe what was happening as to regards to the Islands they literally had to rub their eyes in total disbelief to the British Governments stance regarding the Islands. The British government were seemingly undoing decades of government policy within eighteen months of coming to power. The issue in parliament was the government had been elected with a majority seat in parliament the opposition could not form a majority with any of the opposition parties. Meanwhile China had much sway within some of the African states be it in the mining for natural recourses or for oil. The country also had a lot of influence in Pakistan and it was helping to bolster road, rail and electricity production. There was a project to link Pakistan with China, via a massive transport network. To the disgust of India and the United States. World politics was changing at a rapid pace and it became very difficult to keep apace. The pacific region was extremely unpredictable especially North Korea having fired more ballistic missiles like someone setting off fireworks in their back garden and not knowing where the fireworks would end up. The world was like the song "mad world" if an alien in outer space could look down on the world they would no doubt think all humans were crazy and mad. In Brussels Emile and Bertrand were sat on their own in their local bar talking about world politics and the current state of Britain also the plight of its armed forces. Bertrand commented on the fact that a group of meek politicians including civil servants were practically destroying such a great nations military power and it was something the Nazi's were never able to do during the second world war. He also referred to Lord Nelson and the duke of Wellington saying the great men would be turning in their graves if they could see what was happening to their great country, a nation they had helped to defend one with his life. Bertrand began to laugh and when he said he thought he could hear Winston Churchill shouting in anger from beyond the grave. After Emile took a sip of beer he said, "if only there was something we could do to stop the mad things happening to Britain" Bertrand warned him against getting involved in anything stupid. Emile hadn't heard what his friend said he was miles away deep in his thoughts. He was wandering if the group could come up with any ideas to say mobilise many veterans to protest the British Government. His immediate thought was to protest at the European parliament? He wasn't thinking straight possibly from years of drinking and very strong alcohol who knows. In America Sam was sat in his bed sit, drinking bourbon at the same time he was watching the CNN, American news channel" there was some news coverage of the NATO summit in Belgium. The reporter was clarifying the various rumours of the British government's and its refusal to commit to remaining within NATO. Suddenly on hearing the breaking news Sam began to swear at the TV and he was feeling very angry at the news of the British PM possibly pulling the country out of NATO. Sam knew it would be an extremely and foolish thing for Britain to do. He suddenly shouted, "what the fuck is next" he was by now extremely wound up he poured himself a very large bourbon. In Belgium the bar manager in the bar Emile was sat in switched on the news channel and the Belgium news station was also covering the NATO summit. The Belgium news reporter broke the same news regarding there was a very strong possibility of Britain pulling out of NATO. A defence spokesman gave his point of view regarding the ramifications for NATO if Britain did decide to pull out of the alliance. Bertrand turned to Emile and said, "bloody hell the world has truly gone fucking mad". He then replied, "but surely they can't do that can they"? just then the rest of the drinking "gang" turned up and said almost in unison "have you heard the bloody news"? Emile said, "oh yes we have" someone said, "what the fuck is going on" Bertrand responded, "the mad have truly inherited the world". Meanwhile inside the NATO summit the secretary general and the President of the United States forcefully demanded the British PM attend a private meeting prior to the signing of the alliance. The document would have ratified the treaty and it would allow for much more joint military cooperation for each member state. The PM knew exactly what was coming up and, so he had been prepared for the onslaught from both men. The PM was strategically sat next to the secretary general the President of the USA was strategically sat at the head of the table. The president didn't mess around with his words and he asked the PM directly "is Britain pulling out of NATO"? The PM's reply was just as blunt "yes". The secretary general responded, "but it's just bloody madness it is suicidal to do so". The Presidents response was "goddamit you are leaving your country without any form of defence you will be naked & open to any attack from any tom dick and harry". The Prime minister calmly said, "I realise that, but my government has been elected by the British people on a non-nuclear and a neutral status mandate and this is just what I intend doing and I am sticking by my promise I made to the people in the country". The president stood up and walked out of the room and slammed the door by the time the secretary general and the British PM finished talking the president suddenly called for an impromptu press conference where he announced after sixty nine years of the NATO alliance he was deeply saddened to confirm Britain was now walking out of the NATO alliance, a hush descended inside the room and the gathered journalists were dumfounded about the hot off the press news he went on to explain even further to all those gathered he had just left a private meeting with the British PM , the secretary general explained it was recently confirmed by the PM Britain was leaving the alliance very soon rather than later. Meanwhile the PM walked out of the main conference room via a different route to where the President was still giving a press conference. He was stood in the main conference room with the other heads of states the President was the first leader to sign his countries commitment to NATO he noticed the British PM's name was neatly crossed off the document. The remaining leaders walked up to the table and duly signed their countries allegiance to the alliance. The PM walked out of the conference hall and as he did so he tried to walk past the press gathering in the hall and without being spotted by the press, but inevitably he had been spotted by members of the press pack. Not many of the foreign press corps would have easily recognised the British Prime Minister just by his attire as he was wearing a suit with a tank top white shirt and a red tie and he looked just like any normal person and not statesman. He was called over to provide a press statement and as he stood in front of the world's press he began to inform the world "it has been an historic meeting and I am proud to have led Britain out of the NATO Alliance as promised in my governments manifesto I hope to ratify at the UN council in New York Britain was to become a neutral country like Switzerland and Sweden". He walked out of the building and into his diplomatic car and headed for the British Embassy. Leaving behind a gaggle of bemused press most could not believe what was said the PM had confirmed exactly what the President had mentioned in his short press conference. The American President was livid at the post press meeting and he had to bite his tongue and all he could say was "I am very sad a staunch ally of America, Europe and NATO has decided to leave the organisation and with that he left the building. Inside his limousine he picked up the handset on his encrypted phone and he contacted his Défense Secretary who hadn't travelled with the President, he already knew the British would pull out of NATO the President required his Défense secretary who was sat in the pentagon. The president told the secretary to immediately withdrawal all military support and all cooperation with Great Britain. The secretary was informed to start the drawdown of US military installations from Britain and to cease all military intelligence cooperation with the British Intelligence agencies. In Russia the president could not contain his joy at the recent news. Those around the president had never seen him so happy and in fact he was ecstatic. In Britain those in the military could not quite believe what just happened at the NATO meeting as it was unprecedented within the annuals of military history and cooperation. Some of the more senior military commanders resigned from their posts. The British secretary of defence was unconcerned at their resignations. The government wanted a defence review and a defence white paper to reduce the size of the British Armed Forces the government wanted even more and deeper cuts, the Armed forces were already cut to the bone? The

Royal Navy recently commissioned two aircraft carriers into service there was already talk of one of aircraft carriers being sold off and its crew moved to other roles within the Royal Navy and some personnel were to be made redundant much of this was only hearsay. The PM decided the Army was far too large and expensive with the government's policy to turn the United Kingdom into a neutral country there was no need to have such a large Armed Forces or a large standing Army that would have no overseas role if the PM ever got his way. There were whispers in Whitehall the Russian Navy would like to get their hands on one of the Royal Navy latest aircraft carries. In the end the sale went ahead, America purchased the vessel they moth balled the carrier. Many in the Royal Navy breathed a sigh of relief when the Americans purchased the vessel. Both China and Russia showed a lot of interest in the purchase of the vessel. The Russians were more than happy at the British governments disassembly of the British Militaries capability to thwart any future military attack on the country. To very many people the British government were only carrying out was contained in the leftist party's election manifesto policy they were sticking to the many pledges they spouted to the public about during the last election. The government were democratically elected and there wasn't much anything could be done to reverse the people's decision made in the election. But at the same time the government were seen to be dismantling many of the countries historic institutions the government was hell bent on changing British history and what the country's history had stood for in the world. Within the government there were some extremely far left minded members of the current cabinet, some of whom had their own agendas. On the 6th of June 2019 the French and Americans wanted to commemorate 75 five years since D Day on the 6th June 1944. There were still some military veterans who were alive and survived D Day many of the veterans were in their nineties some were centenarians one hundred years or older. The only ally who did not believe in celebrating war or for that matter any armed conflict was the British government. To the disappointment of the other allies who were involved in the invasion of Europe in 1944. Britain officially turned down the country's invite to officially attend the many ceremonies to mark such an historic occasion. The French and the Americans had taken the refusal as a major diplomatic snub. The news was soon leaked to the worlds press regarding the British government's snub at an historic occasion and it would never be repeated because many of those who fought on the beaches of France would have died. The Royal British Legion soon mustered a campaign for every British Military Veteran to travel to France and to privately celebrate the occasion Including British Military Veterans from every conflict and war since the second world war. The British government forbade any serving British Regiment from attending the D Day celebrations over in France. Many of the war re-enactment organisations loaded their military vehicles onto cross-channel ships heading for France. Also, every replica and restored Royal Naval vessel sailed across the channel to join in the celebrations. Many of the restored and privately-owned RAF aircraft also flew over to the many small French airfields to join in the D Day celebrations. It was a nation's reaction to the government's reluctance to commemorate the historic invasion of Europe and subsequent freedom from the Nazi's iron grip on Europe. Many people in the UK were extremely embarrassed at the governments leftist stance at snubbing the D Day memorial events in France it was all too much for many British people. It seemed to many people as though the government was embarrassed at the nation's great military past and was trying its best to eradicate the countries historic past and its culture. The government wished to celebrate other cultures and lesser known people of the world. Many traditional statues around the country were removed to the anger of many people. The government wanted every village and town to tear down their war monument's, but it was a step too far for so many people to take and there was a revolt in parliament it had forced the government to back down and as such all the war monuments across the country remained in place. A member of the opposition in parliament declared the country was being run just like a banana republic. The Bank of England also warned the opposition leader the government was close to spending the remainder of the countries gold reserve. The shadow chancellor was extremely concerned because he and the Bank of England governor knew the treasury were "dipping" into the countries gold reserves. The governor of the Bank of England was independent of government and as such sent a detailed report to both the chancellor of the exchequer and his counterpart. The current government in a very short time managed to cut its ties with many of its allies and security organisations. On the home front inflation was rocketing and out of control. Many of the reasons could be laid at the foot government's security policies and its withdrawal from many international alliances the food blockade was the major reason on the state of the country and food prices soared in price. Since the previous government pulled out of European union some food prices soon began to rise in price. Since the current government came to power almost anything which was imported into the country had also come with a very high price, they increased the VAT, Value Added Tax, on every product purchased. America curtailed its supply of wheat and cereal to Britain. The British government knew they were up against things more especially trying to feed the population of Britain. Food was becoming increasingly expensive and some foods were rare at the supermarkets. Meanwhile the FSB "planted" a fictitious military veteran on FSB and was accepted to join the veterans group. His name was Andrei and he was meant to be a veteran of the Syrian war. Andrei obviously did have a great deal of knowledge of the Russian military and he could easily bluff his way on FB no one would be any wiser. "Andrei" was deliberately kept in the background on the social media site for now? His access to the group would become relevant at a later stage. The FSB did not wish to show its hand too early. George posted some messages on Social media regarding the upcoming D Day commemorations and how disgusted he was at the British governments recent announcement of its nonattendance at the commemorations over in France. George announced he would be attending the various memorials on his own. Some French and Canadian veterans were attending alongside Emile and Bertrand. They agreed to meet alongside what was Gold beach in France. There was yet another veteran who also wanted to meet with the other veterans and his name was Kurt the German military veteran. Kurt was quiet recently on the social media site and whenever he posted anything on the site any of his subject matter wasn't interesting and it was typically Germanic and very boring. They all agreed to meet in Normandy and at a café in the seaside town of Arromanches the town is situated on the western edge of what was known during the second world war as Gold beach. It was the beach the British 50th Division had to take and fully intact on the 6th June 1944. The veterans agreed to meet on Thursday 6th June 2019 in a little over 18 months' time. During the main event there would be almost every European head of state less the British Prime minister. His government's decision placed the British Royal family in a very difficult position, much to the glee of the Prime Minister.

Hesitant

Chapter 5 – Bad Governance

Meanwhile the main British opposition party was attempting to forge alliances with the other opposition parties with a mind to form a more powerful opposition to the British government. It wasn't an easy task it was proving very difficult to get the other opposition parties on board as each party held its own political agenda with their own political beliefs. The PM soon realised what was happening regarding the opposition parties he was more than happy the opposition to his government wasn't going the way the opposition wanted things to go. At the same time, he knew his government were proving to be extremely unpopular with the public and all because of his government's ludicrous and out of date policies and his own ideas. Inflation was by now rampant many ordinary people's pension pots were shrinking and pensions weren't keeping up with inflation. Certain foods had by now disappeared from the supermarket shelves it was all down to the American trade and food blockade of Britain. The reason for the blockade was because of the governments wish to turn the country into a neutral nation and a sort of utopia state. The Russian government recently approached the British Government to offer financial assistance at such a difficult time. They offered technical assistance the assistance was to only provide help and technical assistance to help destroy Britain's nuclear arsenal including the many nuclear reactors currently housed in seven nuclear plants around the country. The UK has fifteen operational nuclear reactors along with the many tons of nuclear waste produced in the nuclear plants the government were totally against keeping any nuclear weapons including nuclear power stations. Much more worrying for the Americans due to getting wind of Russia's recent approach to the British government the Americans were so concerned about Britain's nuclear-powered submarines and the submarines compliments of nuclear warheads and there was no way on earth the Russians would be allowed to get access to the subs. The British government seemed to have within just a couple of years to have helped to bring the country to its knees. The head of the IMF, the International Monetary Fund also wrote to the British government warning the PM that in their professional view Britain would be bankrupt within four years at the most and if not sooner. They could not foresee any future growth, but they knew the country's gold reserve would very soon be spent. The world bank refused to bail out the UK's finances because the PM had been previously warned by the world bank to cease issuing more Gilt bonds, Gilts are bonds are issued by the British government and are issued in £100 units, the bonds promise to pay a fixed income over a fixed term. The IMF could not tell a country what to do but they are aware of the world's financial markets and the organisation is acutely aware of a countries financial institutions and just how healthy a country's finances are, the IMF is an extremely influential body within the world of finance. They can predict if a country is unable to pay its outstanding debts long before it ever becomes common knowledge to the stock markets and other trading establishments across the world. The chancellor of the exchequer was planning on saving billions of pounds by reducing the country's military budget and to "sell" off its nuclear submarine fleet and most of the Royal Navies fleet and this was only the start of things to come. At the same time the government had an eye on the countries overseas dependencies including the overseas territories there are currently fourteen under the jurisdiction of the United Kingdom.

The prime minister personally wanted to cut the dependencies and territories adrift and for them to fend for themselves, he concluded the territories and dependencies were a hangover from Britain's colonial past and he had it in mind to make them fend for themselves it would then allow the government to make huge monetary savings. Britain's gold reserves were by now almost non-existent there was talk within the corridors of Whitehall of further tax rises including council tax and because the government had recently reduced central government's payments to every local council. Each citizen across the nation was by now feeling the pinch more especially on their personal finances more so the poor within society, the dream of voting for a fairer government who were full of promises soon turned into the people's worst nightmare. The PM was by now looking very closely at the benefits system he thought his chancellor could cut even more from the huge benefits bill. He was still reluctant to touch the overseas aid budget and it was by now worth billions of pounds. His government were more than happy to "screw" even more out of its own people and yet it was more than happy to fritter away billions of pounds to obscure overseas projects, if the British public knew about the corruption surrounding the overseas aid budget they would have been up in arms. At the same time the leaders from many countries who in receipt of the aid, were sat rubbing their hands with glee yet there were others who could not believe how a country such as Britain could hand over so much money and still squeeze even more money from of its own people and then to hand out the money to many corrupt governments some of the countries receiving the money hated everything Britain stood for. The PM was putting together more legislation to enable Scotland to have a second independence referendum. It was exactly what the Scottish first minister dreamt about, she did not have to do anything apart from stepping back and letting the Prime Minister carry on the way he was going. Many people in the country were dreading Scottish independence, it was as though the government were hell bent on destroying Britain from within, some people were overjoyed, and they could not wait for the outcome or even the demise of such a great nation. There was a major constitutional issue he wanted to address it head on. It was well known the PM had many republican leanings and he wanted to tackle the privy purse. The sovereigns grant is calculated as a percentage of the crown estate in 2016-2017 the grant equated to the cost of 65p per person in the United Kingdom. The government did not believe in the sovereign grant and was contemplating the Royal family to live off the profits from their private investments including the land the family currently owned and much of which is out of bounds to the public. The chancellor of the day recommended to the Queens private secretary for him to gently suggest to HM Queen Elizabeth II to sell some of the Royal family's properties including the many estates and the vast acres of land they own or to make their assets pay their lifestyle. The private secretary suggested to the chancellor it was for him to personally tell Her Majesty with that he quickly left the Chancellors Office and with a very broad smile on his face, he thought to himself "I am not doing the bloody governments dirty work for them". Let's just say he wasn't a great fan of the current incumbents who were in government. The private secretary worked for the Queen over many years he knew how to let her know whatever was being proposed without it ever formally coming from his office. At that precise moment the government began to reduce the defence budget and began the process of slashing what left of the Armed Services to the bone.

Some of the governments many other hair brained ideas were still on the drawing board, so to speak but at the same time there were some drastic and radical proposals which could cause some strong opposition. The country was rapidly running out of money and they were coming up with more and more drastic measures to stem the "bleeding" of funds. The governments "open door" policy to let the thousands refugees and immigrants freely enter the country without carrying out any checks or even to count how many were entering the country was causing so many issues, there was no one in any of the government departments who knew exactly how many people entered the country all of the refugees living rough in camps in and around Calais and Paris over in France were by now empty and it was a similar situation at the port of Dunkirk. All because not one of the British government departments knew how many arrived in the country the government and they could not complete forward planning or even predict the future planning of schools, housing, hospitals they could not accurately plan for the future of the country, the recent census was virtually null and void due to the massive and unaccounted influx of people into the country. In the past the national census allowed various government departments to predict with the aid of computer modelling just many schools, hospitals and housing would be required for the future generations. The country seemed to be on a rocky voyage, some would say it was a voyage into the abys. The chancellor was unable to accurately predict the countries tax revenue nor exactly how much was required to be set aside for social housing and future state benefits or the State pension let alone the country's GDP. There was far too many people living in the country and it was all because of the recent influx of refugees and migrants into the country the country's social services could not predict the recourses required to cope for the many recent arrivals they knew full well it would be top heavy, as more people would require social assistance and including benefits housing etc one of the biggest burdens was none of the recent arrivals will have paid into the UK Tax system, and yes the state would obviously be there to help them and it would mean those currently working in the UK would inevitably see their taxes hiked up to help to financially cover the needs of the many additional people and it would continue for many decades to come and by now the country was creaking at the seams. Many of the refugees and immigrants were monetary migrants and were immediately placing a massive strain on the countries public services and so much more especially trying to just house those additional people dumped onto local authorities who already had so many people already waiting many years for council housing and then finding themselves at the bottom of their local authorities housing ladder. A dictate from central government had decreed refugees and migrants were to be found accommodation immediately none of the refugees or the migrants had any documentation on their possession, in some cases it was a deliberate ploy, because they knew not to carry any official documentation many unscrupulous people were jumping the housing queue to the immense annoyance of local people and their tempers were beginning to fray in those areas the immigrants were sent to, to be housed. There was no control of who was genuine or not. There was a growing resentment and anger bubbling away within the country. It is like everything when there is a "fluid" border system? Some International terrorists managed to slip through the non-existent border checks into the country without a single basic check having been carried out. The situation only helped to add even more stress and strain within the country. In some places where a family almost got to the top of a council housing list were suddenly told they had "slipped" down the housing list and many of the councils scared to say it was because they were told, and sometimes almost ordered, by central government to house needy immigrants and refugees. The councils knew if they did so it would cause consternation by the people who were on the housing lists for years. The PM at the same time was considering hosting a conference within the Palace of Westminster he was hosting some of the more dubious groups in the world who in the past paid the PM's party let's just say "funds" there were some people who would go even further and say it was dirty money paid with the blood of others. At the same time many world leaders were still helping to create much instability and there was much uncertainty in the world it became a place of threats and counter threats and brinkmanship the world had become a place of so much volatility more so than during the cold war. There was so much subterfuge and mistrust many governments were deceiving their own people, much like the current British government.

The rate of inflation in Britain rocketed and mortgages were rising at an alarming rate the interest rate rose several times over with the past eighteen months. Much was due to America having imposed the food embargo and UK food prices were sky high. The PM who when not working was attended his own allotment within central London, he was soon pushing for the UK's population to dig up their gardens and waste land to grow more of their own food he wanted most households to be self-sufficient in growing vegetables. The Department for Environment, Food and Rural Affairs even produced many "grow" your own posters and films on how to grow vegetable produce. It was all very reminiscent of the "dig" for Britain PR campaign used during the second world war for the people of Britain to grow their own food due to the NAZI's submarine blockade of Britain in the second world war and the sinking of merchant shipping bringing food across the Atlantic from America. Within eighteen months the government destroyed much of the country's banking industry, food imports, trade and security and they had managed to sell off much of the country's gold reserve. As mentioned the PM and the chancellor of the exchequer ignored the IMFs, International Monetary Fund, dire warnings regarding the dismal state of Britain's economy. Life for the average person was becoming an uphill struggle and with no end in sight life became a drudgery of "just" getting by in some cases just scraping a living. The president of the USA was incredulous when he got wind of the British governments proposal of hosting a "peace" conference It wasn't a conference of free thinking or democratically elected governments of the world. The British government was proposing to invite many of the world's terrorist leadership. The American president at one stage seriously considered somehow blowing up the conference venue where all the delegates were to gather. His defence staff even seriously considered moving one of Americas aircraft carriers into international waters just off the coast of Britain and using the carriers attack aircraft to bomb the venue. There was one major flaw in the plan and it was the British Prime Minister was democratically elected as leader of a free nation and ok the "special" relationship had all but disappeared but and it was a big, but America could not afford to be seen an assassin of a free and democratically elected leaders of the free world? That would have to be left to for others to do. The government was ruffling many other countries feathers all due to its far-left policies. Also due to its open-door policies regarding immigration there were so many strains on the countries resources. As mentioned the government hadn't recorded the huge influx of people into the country it ended up a free for all. In America Sam was extremely angry at his president who in his eyes seemed to be more and more extreme in his method of governing the country. The Russian president was ecstatic at the British government's decision to withdraw from NATO and for taking British troops, Navy and air force out of the alliance more importantly from the various bases in the Baltic and other eastern European border areas close to Russia. The Russian president could not have done a better job himself even if he tried. Getting back to the international war veterans social media group and so many were angry at the British government's stance on so many security issues. The group was a little less verrucous lately hence why the FSB who were monitoring the group and hadn't recorded much chit chat online. But the FSB had taken its "eye" off what was happening in the UK because it suited the Russians own self-destruction as they saw it. But many unseen things and actions were just bubbling away under the radar. Mainly in the areas the Russians could not observe or monitor no one nation can ever gauge the mood of another nation from afar. A picture of a nation cannot be gauged by disgruntled nationals on a social media platform. Individuals can be monitored with the sole aim of possibly using them to surreptitiously or using them for some "dirty" work in the future. Meanwhile Emile and Bertrand formed their own far fight political views on where they thought Belgium should be heading, politically that was. They secretly campaigned on the splitting up of Belgium into two separate countries one half the French speaking part of the country going it alone and having much stronger trade and a banking closeness with France. They also thought very strongly of casting the Flemish speaking part of the country to its own devices and to leave it fending for itself. It was almost as though the pair were living in the past. The French speaking Rexist party who were a fascist party and joined forces with the NAZI occupation of Belgium. In Britain it was well known in various International governments that Britain would do nothing if another country decided to sail their warships into British sovereign waters.

Many NATO countries were extremely worried about the ongoing British military situation and the government's determination to do away with the military. France "stationed" a few of its own fleet just within British waters including Norway it was to counter any possible threat from Russia. America was already covering Britain's responsibility by stationing Nuclear submarines and guarding the Atlantic from Russian submarines or their surface fleet from making a "run" for it in the Atlantic. The British government ignored any protestations made by other nations, regarding the countries reluctance to adhere to its security obligations. The government were already showing its true intent towards the nation's taxes. There was very little of the countries gold reserve remaining and, so it was left for the local authorities at county council level to "plug" the gap hence the increase local authority's council tax. The chancellor "hiked" up the financial districts taxes and off loaded the responsibility from central government. Overseas aid increased two-fold and it was still helping to fund so called terrorist umbrella organisations. The Armed forces were at an all-time low there hadn't been any investment in military manpower or material and moral was at an all-time low, there was no light at the end of the tunnel. In America congress and the president of the United States virtually referred to UK a rogue state run by mad men. It wasn't a vote of confidence. The Russian ambassador in London delivered a letter to the Prime minister's office at number 10 downing street. The letter was from the Russian president requesting the use of British ports for the sole use of refuelling its naval fleet whenever it was in British waters. The PM and the defence secretary replied by stating they would have to have a little more time to consider the Russian president's request. The government did not at the time have a well thought through foreign policy the country's foreign policy was in tatters and it seemed to others in some quarters Britain's foreign policy was written on the back of a fag packet. The British government was in power for just over two years the country seemed to many of those who elected them into government on a downward spiral without any breaks to help slow the disastrous governorship down. The parliamentary opposition still hadn't managed to mount a strong opposition, nor did they manage to form a strong alliance with any of the other parties within parliament. Cuba received much of the British overseas aid and Castro's brother had recently passed away and the British PM attended his funeral Cuba recently elected a new president who was a staunch communist on taken up power in the country he already started negotiations with Russia for both military assistance and monetary aid. The move seriously alarmed the Americans. Once again Russia was slowly beginning to expand its influence across the far side of the globe. Getting back to Europe, NATO could not accept Britain ever being used as an aircraft carrier for the Russians. The pentagon and the white house drew up plans to try and stop Britain from being used by Russia as a huge Russian military base as the Americans had done during the cold war. France was extremely worried about the growing influence of

Russia with the British government. The political situation within Britain and the rest of the world was plummeting by the day. Sam was by now in constant contact with George over in London via social media Sam had been berating George over the British PM's and his cronies all George could do was to agree with everything Sam was saying because he didn't have an answer to counter Sam's digging at the government. It was at this point George stated if he only he could get his hands on a sniper's rifle he would soon "take out" the British PM. It was just what Sam wanted to hear and the FSB also made a note of the conversation. What was said was soon transcribed the content was then despatched to Moscow. In Moscow the conversation was seen in a favourable light and it was something else the FSB could then pass onto the British government more especially George's thoughts and having been identified as a potential assassin, but he wasn't the only person in Britain who also felt this way. It was fast approaching June 2019 and a year of events to commemorate the D Day landings on the June sixth, 1944 to commemorate the successful invasion of fortress Europe and to help free the people of Europe from the tyranny of NAZI Germany. The Prime Minister stuck to his word and to not attend the D Day celebrations. The Royal family were attending and would attend in force there were many Royals who the British public never heard of or seen in public. It was the British Royal families show of strength and their feelings towards the British governments puny and disrespectful stance regarding the D Day memorial. Even though the Ministry of Defence forbade all serving military personnel from attending the events there were many service personnel who attended they took official leave to attend the events in a private capacity. There were thousands of military veterans who also attending. At the Gold beach area of Arromanches and Kurt was good as his word and met Emile and

Bertrand at a local café near the sea front the pair felt it was slightly strange and he wanted to meet them. When Kurt turned up what struck the pair he was so much younger looking than they thought he would look. The pair already had a few drinks prior to Kurt's arrival and when he arrived at the cafe he mentioned to the pair he didn't drink alcohol but instead he drank a cup of coffee. After they introduced themselves to one another he told them he was looking forward to seeing the ceremony on the 6th of June. He was carrying a camera case and when Emile asked to look at the camera he was impressed at the camera it looked very professional he asked Kurt if he was a professional cameraman and he replied, "oh no" he was just a keen amateur photographer.

The French government were seriously considering withdrawing all diplomatic contact with Britain in diplomatic terms it was a serious move on behalf of France and it isn't something which is taken lightly. The president of America was never going to remove his country's diplomatic contact with Great Britain. It was like the adage "keep your enemies close and your friends even closer". For in the president's mind Britain at the time had been hijacked by its politicians and at some point, the people would eventually come to their senses and he had much faith in the people of the UK. The world at the same time was extremely unpredictable and people including businesses could not plan a future for themselves or their families yet only ten years previously the future had seemed very stable and, in some cases, very rosy. The many financial mandarins were becoming nervous, because their financial models had been a complete and utter waste of time. The pound was on the slide but in a downwards direction. In china the yen seemed to be on a war footing it had much to do with Americas obsession with North Korea and china turned many atolls in around the china seas and far afield into military bases miniature aircraft carriers and its industry switched production to building war material. The British were only a small cog in the wider world and China could so easily throw the tracks out of sequence and cause things within the country to grind to halt. Just a tiny cog in a much larger cog in the workings of the world's economy. The public in Britain were experiencing and enduring Americas food blockade was beginning to bite hard. On top of the many tax rises which were heaped upon the population. The chancellor was also heaping so much corporation tax on British companies as such many recently left the UK and for Germany based out of Hamburg. It had become far too expensive to be based in London. Some companies just left a skeleton staff in London, in hope of things in London would improve sometime in the future, perhaps? Many businesses moved away from London to save company profits and to grow their businesses even if they were based outside of the UK, it had made far more financial sense. Britain had by now left the European Union, EU after the 2017 EU referendum, it enabled Britain to leave the EU. The country absorbed the ramifications of leaving but the country was trying to absorb the body blows from its own government nobody could forecast what the government of the day would do next. The financial sector could not predict the country's financial future anymore because it was impossible to predict any fiscal government policies, as they didn't seem to have any policies. Unfettered immigration into the country was taking its toll and many who had lived in the UK and for a long time it now felt as though immigration and the huge influx of refugees was now putting far too much of a strain on all the countries recourses. Many families had for generations paid into the "system" with their taxes to support the countries support services such as schooling, hospitals and housing and the influx of immigrants etc placed such a burden on the countries tax system the coffers were by now empty. At the D Day celebrations Emile and Bertrand at last met Kurt taking photographs of various dignitaries and members of European Royal families they had noticed him clicking away with his camera when suddenly members of the US president's close protection security team frog marched Kurt towards members of the French gendarme, police. For Emile and Bertrand, the scene was comical, and they could not stop laughing because Kurt came across to them as a cold fish and he kept himself to himself he wasn't spontaneous or funny but watching the scene unfold before them was very comical. The American government had a mole working at No10 Downing Street, The Prime Minister's office, the mole was against the governments communist theories and more especially their policies and believed after 24 months in power they virtually brought the country to its knees, a country she loved dearly. She managed to photo copy some very sensitive documents one of which was the full contents of Russia's request to use the many British ports to base and to refuel Russian naval ships. The Americans received many a leaked report of the Russians request to Britain, but they had never seen the full transcript and now the mole sent them the full transcript and with the British Prime minister's handwritten comments, it allowed the Americans to know how the Prime minister was thinking by reading his hand-written notes. It hadn't been so much the letter it was more the fact the Americans finally had a willing mole at the heart of the British government and she was working at Number 10 Downing Street the mole was a contact with whom they were able to access certain sensitive documents. The home secretary was a hands-on politician he wanted to curtail both MI5 and MI6's influence, he reduced both departments budgets to both director's dismay. The prime minister in the past a file opened on him by both departments because in his youth the Prime Minister as a young politician made links to and Irish terrorist group and other devious terrorist organisations. MI5 is the domestic counter intelligence agency and its mission is to keep the country safe. The head of MI5 recently submitted a report to the home secretary about the abandonment of border controls and the lack of vetting of the many thousands of refugees and migrants who recently flooded into the country and he had pointed out that his agents knew of many hundreds of potential terrorists. The home secretary submitted a cost cutting requirement to the heads of both MI5 and MI6 to reduce costs and if need be the departments might be required to move at short notice from the current MI5 and MI6 buildings, Thames House a grade II listed building in Millbank in London, and to move into the MI6 building on the embankment in Vauxhall London. The MI5 bureau chief felt as though he was banging his head against a brick wall his agents recently identified a serious terrorist threat to the UK because many of the potential terrorists hoodwinked the British authorities and subsequently crossed into the country unchallenged with the hordes of refugees and migrants without having any checks carried out. Some had even been housed and made welcome by the British tax payer. But these people only had one thing on their minds and it was how to integrate into British society and then plan a "spectacular" terrorist attack and to kill and maim as many people as they could. Terrorists do not care who they kill be it women, children, men, or religion they are indiscriminate when they carry out acts of terrorism they are cowards. The home secretary was of a Marxist persuasion and believed if everyone is treated with the same respect and humanity and compassion then the whole population would be content with their lot. But the problem with his philosophy the country's wealth is spread so thinly and is almost worthless in the end. Those who wanted to kill British people have no compassion of respect for life. The President of America may have got it right when he referred to Britain as a banana republic. He was adamant in the house of congress when he announced that America would not loan the UK further finance to help prop up the pound nor would he authorise any further financial bail outs. The president recently called into the oval office many of the CEO's who were operating in the financial districts of New York city and he called in the CEO's from wall street itself. He wanted all of them to ensure the UK was not given authority for any further credit, these were the most powerful financial people in the world. If his government found that any US based companies were helping to bail out the UK government if any financial company were ever caught he would personally revoked that companies financial trading licenses. After satisfying himself that the financial sector in the US was in no doubt of what he wanted he could confidently put even more pressure on the UK government.

Since leaving the EU the UK could not ask the EU for any financial assistance it would be out of the question and besides the current British government were detested in Europe. The British prime minister only had one other option open to him and it was to approach the Russian President. The president already requested the use of British ports, so his Naval fleet could resupply and fuel at the ports. But there was one other request he had, and it was to use some of Britain's almost redundant military airbases. The prime minister wanted to try and find some source of funding perhaps a quick method of receiving finances from another country especially since the American congress switched off the money tap. Russia seemed a very good source of revenue for the treasury and furthermore revenue. At the same time there was so much happening both in the UK and elsewhere in the world. No government could trust one another it was a dark place. The Russians thought the British government was very week indeed and just ripe for the plucking. It was a just assumption because the British were very weak a lot weaker than the Russians and Americans could ever dream of. It was during this background of political uncertainty gripping both Britain and the world. America had become extremely concerned at Britain and at its reluctance to adhere to its military commitments by the government's commitment to withdraw from many major worldwide treaties. The government wanted another Defence Review to consider the country pulling out of NATO including its nuclear submarine commitments. The thinking behind the Defence Review was to reduce the country's military manpower across all three of the Armed Forces. The government wanted to reduce the defence budget even further. The "mole" at No10 had managed to download a copy of the Defence Review document and to send a copy to her contact in the American Défense Department who she knew would forward the document to the Défense Secretary. Meanwhile Russian forces were soon ready to deploy nuclear weapons in the Crimea and Kaliningrad in the Baltic an area neighbouring Poland. America was still of the opinion the British public would soon have to come to its senses and see just what the British government were up to and they would eventually vote the government out of power and reinstate themselves back into NATO before it became too late. The American president thought if it came to a third world war Britain would not be able to just stand aside and watch on the side lines. He thought to himself the many people who were recently greeted in Britain with open arms would turn their backs on the British as they would not be willing to serve in the British armed forces at a time of war and could leave a sizable fifth column on Britain's streets. The Prime Minister wanted to reduce the military budget and to put some of the savings into the overseas aid budget. He also wanted to plough some of the savings into the NHS, elderly care and Education. A noble gesture if in normal times but these were not "normal" times. China also approached the government of the day and they suggested a most favourable offer by investing large sums of money into Britain.   China's interest regarding the investment in Britain was kept secret because in the governments cash strapped eyes it seemed very tempting. News soon came to the ears of the chancellor the countries gold reserve had finally run out as the saying goes "the cupboard was bare". The prime minister was somewhat alarmed but not that shocked. The American president was acutely aware of the financial situation in Britain, the American Embassy in London was keeping him up to date. So was the reliable "mole" working in No10.   In Moscow, the FSB also knew about the social and financial happenings in London.   The Russian president was considering selling gold to the UK on a long lease loan period, another option was to pay the rent for the use of British ports and airfields with gold.   China was about to get themselves a foothold in Europe possibly within the UK by basing its military aircraft and warships in Britain for cash they knew the UK government were in dire need of cash or gold it didn't matter which. America was aware of both Russia and China's serious interests in the UK and its facilities. The prime minister's dream of a utopia was rapidly disappearing, and it was now rapidly turning into a nightmare. His government and more so his own vision of turning Britain into a neutral country was dead in the water. His government's policies and were a throwback to the nineteen seventies and not a twenty first century society. The country seemed to a lot of people as having been sold off to the highest bidder. What was ironic Britain was sending some of the overseas aid budget to china?? To George who was sat inside his bedsit knew nothing of the catastrophe soon facing the country. What he did know was the cost of the everyday things in life such as food, taxes and more importantly the high cost of food and the lack of food on the shelves it was all due to America's blockade of food stuffs to the UK. It was fast approaching three years the country was by now in dire straits and it would not be too long before the country would be on its knees. The world bank was soon going to call in all the UK's outstanding loans because the bank was extremely concerned that the UK would very soon default on its debts to the rest of the world. It was at this point that the opposition parties finally got their act together and stopped squabbling over inter party politics and to do something to oust the government. They had to come to an agreement for the sake and of the greater interest of the country and to join forces to form a formidable opposition to the government. At last some common sense prevailed on the political front, the insecurity and lack of action lifted in British politics. The political cogs ran slowly and at this precise moment in time it could be just the saving of the country, the people had enough of politics, taxes and a government who seemed to be more concerned about the past and not on the future.

In Germany during the same time the previous chancellor fell on her sword and a new far right government was surprisingly elected into power. The last time a far-right party governed the country was in the nineteen thirties it was the NAZI party and of course was headed by Adolf Hitler. In Germany over the past six years Germany seriously struggled to assimilate the @1.5 million refugees and the dynamics of the country totally changed since the masses of refugees having arrived in the country. The current chancellor managed to get a new law passed through the Bundestag, parliament. It was a law to voluntarily return many of the refugees to their country of origin and many willingly took up German citizenship and many fled the past wars in Syria the country was at peace for almost two years and eventually the president was toppled from power and a new President was elected in his place. Billions of dollars were invested in the country to assist in its re-building programme things like the infrastructure and housing. It meant the country would need many of its countrymen and women to return and to help rebuild the country and many who escaped the war were specialists in their field of expertise such as doctors, nurses, engineers and technicians. The country needed many of the young children to return to help build the future as they were Syria's future. So, the German government thought it was the best option for the government to help as many refugees to return home from their adopted country. Not many refugees had wanted to return to Syria. Most over time assimilated into German culture and of course they were fully entitled to the countries benefits and housing system. Most knew if they volunteered to be repatriated to Syria they would not entitled to the same level of state benefits as they were entitled to in Germany. The United Kingdom could not assimilate the massive influx of refugees or immigrants. Tensions within the UK were simmering just below the surface of polite society. The various terrorist groups who managed to slip into the country split into two-man terrorist teams. Each team were housed in various safe houses across the UK. The smugglers moved the teams in pair across the channel for added security none of the teams ever met each other over in France. Weaponry was a major issue as the UK had very strict gun laws, so access to the type of weapons the groups needed weren't so easy to obtain. They could not purchase their weaponry in the UK twenty to thirty years ago they may have been able to purchase such weapons from home grown terrorist organisations such as the IRA, Irish Republican Army. But those days were thankfully over with. The only solution was to smuggle arms and munitions into the UK via boat the ideal place to do so was the south coast, just across the English Channel and France, the south coast was ideal. The groups had terrorist contacts within Paris who could get their hands on a small fast speed boat within the Brittany area of France. Heavy calibre weaponry such as Kalashnikov's and 7.62 mm ammunition were easy to obtain within mainland Europe. The refugee route through Eastern Europe was the ideal place it was where some Eastern bloc countries were selling surplus munitions and tons of plastic explosives for extra cash. Some Eastern European soldiers were being paid a pittance by their armed forces they needed extra cash they also didn't mind where it came from or who it came from. They were more than happy to sell surplus and captured weaponry, including explosives to those who paid well, payments were made in US dollars with no questions asked. It was up to the terrorist suppliers to get the material to the French coast without being caught. Once the supplies were packed onto a boat there was nothing stopping the terrorists or the arms cache landing on a beach somewhere in Southern England as there were no border guards, or immigration and military patrols operating along the wide-open spaces along the southern coast of England and it was all too easy, you might say "plain sailing". Many locals living on the south coast did report many suspicious boats having been found beached on the many south coast beaches, but the authorities still hadn't responded to the many sightings. Many locals soon stopped reporting the illegal landings because of the lack of response by the authorities. This was the route the terrorist groups soon decided to move their lethal weaponry into the UK. Most of the terrorists used and trained overseas with the lethal AK47 assault rifles and it was the favoured terrorist weapon of choice. Each one of the two-man terrorist teams made an encrypted text to a central contact mobile providing an update regarding their current situation within the UK. Many of the teams travelled around the country on scooters and they dressed as any other person, so they didn't stand out from the crowd. They looked non descript and wore bike helmets to help blend in with the crowds and they used mobile phone cameras to take photographs of possible target, this was carried out over many months, they weren't in any rush as time was very much on their side, the security forces didn't have any intelligence on any of the terrorist teams, no one else in the two man teams still didn't know anything about the other team members the only contact was with the team coordinating them, be it via the internet or the pay as you go mobiles. The cells were by now based in the major cities in and around the country. The UK security services were unaware of an impending terrorist plot. The security minister tried to close the gate after the horse had bolted, but it was all far too late all too little too late. He tried resurrecting an idea the previous government wanted to implement, and it was the idea of using part time and retired volunteers to assist the patrolling of the many vulnerable beaches and river inlets on the south coast of England to act as volunteer customs and exercise personnel the idea was eventually scrapped. But there was no sign of any more extra full time, customs and exercise including immigration personnel having been hired to take on the extremely important roles and so the many coastal regions remained open to smugglers, illegal immigrants and terrorists all still arriving undetected and into southern England and undetected. The situation was well known to successive governments not just the current incumbent sat in Number 10. The idea of a volunteer group keeping an eye on the southern coast was on the agenda. Both the terrorists and those wanting to enter the UK had known the coasts of Southern England were wide open and ripe for smuggling people into the UK and there wasn't anything the government were doing about trying to prevent it happening. These were people who even though the official borders were wide open if they were spotted on CCTV, Close circuit television, would be tracked. There were many undesirables wanting to enter the country via the back door. Including those who had wanted to smuggle arms and munitions to spread horror on the streets of the UK. The prime minister soon found himself in a quandary as he sympathised with many of the organisations including terrorist groups who were affiliated to middle east governments who supported state sponsored terrorism. Even more so because some of the UK's overseas aid budget was sent to the same governments and organisations who had links to various undesirable groups. The US president Mark Zoola was very angry at the British Prime Minister Julien Jones. The president was a great fan of the British people but not of the UKs current prime minister. The people of Great Britain wouldn't take too much more higher tax hikes and the very high food prices, or the food embargo still being enforced by the US and more recently Canada who had joined the food embargo of Britain all because of the PM's stupid policies and his ideology. The UK military was reduced to levels not seen since before the first world war. Both the Russians and Chinese were on the side lines wanting to exploit the British governments weaknesses. In Russia's eyes it was looking more like the British

PM was carrying out his own personal vendetta against Britain's elite and it all stemmed from his days as a student.

Chapter 6 – Credit

The time was about right for the exploitation of the veteran's social media group by a foreign secret service organisation. The world at the time was in such a mess both politically and militarily, the British government was prostituting its military assets to the highest bidder. There were a few countries around who were very eager to encourage even more chaos and uncertainty to prevail throughout the world their leaders would like nothing better than to bring anarchy to much of the world and for those leaders to help spread anarchy and to come along and pick up the pieces to install their own values on another nation. Life in some countries was a daily struggle for their own citizens while the elite drank champagne and ate caviar, life for the ordinary people struggling and, on the streets, life was so cheap. The people living in the pariah states do not have the luxury of freedom of speech or religion and most just wanted to escape the poverty and to try and make it to Europe and more especially to the UK, in the west basic freedoms were taken for granted. In fact, the people of the pariah countries were slowly being trampled underfoot and they were ruled by undemocratic dictators. Meanwhile the veteran's social media group was about to be exploited. The FSB by now been monitoring the group for a couple of years and the director of the FSB, based in Moscow nominated a two-man team to come up with a plan to exploit the group for its own political aims. An ex foreign legionnaire who called himself François recently joined the group and he confirmed he had previously served in the French Foreign legion his unit was deployed to Kuwait during the first Gulf War, Afghanistan and central Africa including some of France's former colonies across the world. François was extremely vociferous he liked to air some extremely strong views regarding the current French government. He was totally against France remaining within the European Union, EU. He believed the French should have left the union like Britain did under a Tory government. But his current thinking was he did not have any truck with the current British government because he could see just like many others of how a great country was slowly being destroyed by its own government and in his opinion, it was such a sad thing to happen to a great nation, he thought the government was selling the British people down the river he could not understand why no one in British politics was doing anything about it to stop the madness. François was totally different to most other members of the social media group. He didn't drink, and he kept himself extremely fit he was also member of his local shooting club and would hunt for deer and boar. He was more of a political beast than any of the others on the site. But there was something all those who were members of the social media group had in common with one another. Each one of them were very unhappy with their respective governments. The group was fast becoming a melting pot of different military veteran. In Saint Petersburg Ivor noticed many more of his old comrades from service in Afghanistan who recently joined the group they all had similar stories from their service overseas. He enjoyed contacting them to reminisce about their military service in what was then the "Soviet" army. The FSB head had made a record of those in the group who lived in Russia. The people of Britain were on the verge of bringing down their government because the situation in Britain were getting extremely tough for the ordinary man and woman in the street. Even though the government pushed for the people of Britain to dig up and cultivate each spare piece of land for them to grow fruit and vegetables it just wasn't enough and so it was decided that the park land within most cities was to be turned over to agriculture But it still it wasn't enough to plug the food gap to help feed the, nation, the farmers were working flat out to help feed the country and it just wasn't enough. Within the first year of turning the land over to agriculture nothing grew quick enough it takes a season for crops to begin to grow and to become well established and good enough to be harvested for the following growing year.

The UK's Agricultural Minister needed to source much more of the countries food from far afield such as Africa, Central Europe and South America. The food being imported was costing twice the normal price but nonetheless there was at least some food turning up on the shelves in the supermarkets. The British farmers were extremely hard pressed to produce enough food to feed the nation. Scotland became a giant farmers field so much of the "spare" land was being turned over to growing food and it had to be cultivated. Some of the nation's farmers doubled their stock of cattle it all takes time just over two years to build up the herds. Once again it just wasn't enough. Meat was arriving from New Zealand and Australia the country wasn't starving not just yet at the time it was about surviving the situation, but it couldn't continue this way, and something had to give and very soon. After three years the PM called an emergency cabinet meeting with most of his most senior ministers. His stance and principles as an activist when he was a young politician was all about doing away with nuclear weapons to turn Britain into a neutral country had stuck with him in adult life, his ideology hadn't changed, and his principles remained the same. He was totally against having a large military force and his principles had almost brought the country to its knees. Being a person of principles is all very noble and is all well and good but to run a country into the ground is a disaster waiting to happen. The meeting was for the Prime Minister to tell his ministers he was still going to stick to his guns and he would cease to pay a penny more into the Defence budget only to prop up Britain's nuclear arsenal, instead he would use the money to feed the nation.

On many an occasion George would just sit in his bedsit and vent his anger and frustrations out on the social media site where many of his fellow members sympathised with his views. François sent a public message informing other members of the group that if it was a French government, acting the same way the British government were acting, he would have thought about assassinating the President and Prime Minister of France. It was a very profound statement to make on such a public site, but his remarks had not received a single comment or a single like from other members of the group. Meanwhile at the British governments cabinet meeting the PM addressed those sat around the table he seemed to be in a glum mood. Bearing in mind his cabinet was of his own choosing and every member was politically from the far left also having Marxist sympathies. He finally admitted to those gathered the country was almost on its knees and bankrupt. On that note he opened the chair to allow the chancellor of the exchequer to brief the cabinet on the country's financial state of health and he went on to explain the gold reserve was almost spent and the International Monetary Fund, IMF were about to downgrade the UK's credit rating, meaning it was not good for any further credit. The world bank would not recommend lending the country any more cash. The US were calling in the loans it made to the UK. Hence why the gold reserve was so low. It was because of the loans the US

Credit

wanted the UK to pay back the monies owed and to pay now. The US was beginning to flex its muscles by trying to force the UK back into the bosom of the world, i.e. the US. Most of the cabinet were more than aware of the current situation and were not surprised at all by the financial situation the nation found itself in. The agriculture minister was invited to brief those present on the "way forward" regarding how the country was managing to feed itself. She began by explaining how difficult it was to produce the food the nation had required to feed, itself, she told everyone gathered it also takes a long time to identify the correct land and the soil to cultivate it and to use it and to grow crops to sow the right seed and to then grow and nurture the crop for eventual harvest It takes so much time and labour to harvest the crops. She went on to explain about the countries grain reserves and they were currently very low and would only last another twelve months. The PM invited the Home Secretary to brief the cabinet regarding the current security situation. He began by telling the cabinet that he thought there was growing unrest in the country and it was bubbling away just below the surface the police would not be able to cope with any full scale, unrest. The military had been severely cut, so much so they were at the same strength as the police and would not be able to assist the police if martial law enforced on the people. The home secretary ended his briefing by summarising "the situation would be very dire indeed". The Immigration Secretary was invited to brief the cabinet and it was sobering listening and not for the faint hearted. She began by stating the obvious. She began slowly and explained the country could not sustain the pace of immigration the country was totally and utterly swamped by the vast numbers of immigrants and refugee's flooding the country. The nation's social services had been deluged with calls for assistance and just could not cope with any more refugees and immigrants. She

108

added "I am sorry prime Minister I know what I am about to say conflicts with your moral principles, but enough is enough, if we as a government carry on like this there will be riots on the streets, the likes of we have never seen before in this country". The PM Julien Jones replied, "now we can cope, and we will allow many more refugees and immigrants into our country and that is my final word on the subject I don't want to hear any more about it my mind is made up". The Home Secretary spoke up "we can move more refugees to Scotland, Wales and Northern Ireland and we could if need be, build more housing in the more remote areas of all three countries". Julien the Prime Minister spoke "yes you are right, so ladies and gentlemen nothing is impossible". The Health Secretary spoke up "but Julien the country's infrastructure and more importantly the NHS just cannot cope with the waves of refugees and immigrants entering the country they are arriving with so many different diseases and medical complaints and our hospitals cannot cope with the huge influx the NHS needs vast amounts of investment and many more NHS staff including many more hospitals"?

All those sat around the table knew in their own minds the country required massive investment in the Nation's infrastructure they also knew that there wasn't any more money to be had and so the investment was never going to happen. The country was in a "right" old state. The PM addressed all present and Julien said "as I see things we need to attract investment now not later so we also need to come up with some bloody good ideas and fast, as I see things we only have a few options, we can become a nuclear power once again and allow the US to cease their food blockade and we can once again accept their dirty dollars or be paid by the Russians to allow their armed forces access to British strategic ports and airfields. Or accept payment from both China and Russia to use British air bases including our airspace included in that would be access for both countries to our ports? Or we can continue the way we are heading and bring the country to its knees and bring the wrath of the people of the country on our heads? The choice is ours and ours alone". The PM believed the people of the UK would not care where the money was coming from? He totally misjudged the mood of the British public and he would not be the first or the last Prime Minister of Britain to misjudge the mood of the people. His politics were totally based on the past i.e. the 1970's and mixed with his own version of politics it just hadn't worked in the twenty first century. During the cabinet meeting it boiled down to that lack of finances and to who would bail out the United Kingdom and at what price? The Russian president Anatoly Petrov could not believe just how well politically things were going in Britain. Meaning the country was being run by a bunch of politicians who were living in the past and trying to force their own warped version of politics into the future of the country. Meanwhile in George's local pub in London he was telling the pub landlord he predicted what was currently happing in the UK and the politicians would, as usual ruin the country it would be the ordinary person who would have to pick up the pieces. He sat down at a table with his double scotch and a pint of Guinness, he seemed to drink Guinness and not cider when he drank whisky. Before he had left his bedsit, he posted on the social media network a warning to the others about the downfall of the UK and its Marxist government. While he was sat in the pub he looked at his online post using his mobile phone and he could see he that had received many posts from others regarding his latest comment François made a comment it was on similar lines to his comment about "taking out" the British PM. Life in Britain at the time for most people suddenly become very similar to life in the nineteen forties during and after world war two. Food rationing was the flavour of the day. People in the twenty first century could not believe the country had been reduced to this level of living. To everyone it was alien to them. Many British manufacturing industries had or were contemplating moving to continental Europe.

Anatoly Petrov was in an angry mood as he called on the president of the Russian Federation and the council of ministers. He demanded that they all attend a meeting within the Kremlin. The venue for the meeting was the historic and very symbolic Kremlin senate building housed within the Kremlin grounds in Moscow. The presidents formal title is Mr. President he is the head of the Russian state he is also, the supreme commander in chief of all Russian military forces and he is the holder of the highest office within the Russian Federation. As president he directs the foreign and domestic policy of the Russian federation. He is the comrade supreme commander of the military. The next important politician within the country is the Prime Minister and he is the head of the Russian government he is the second most powerful figure within the Russian federation. As the prime minister and the Russian council of ministers arrived at the rotunda hall which houses the Kremlin Senate building. The hall over many years bore witness to much of Russia's history, the building of the hall began in 1776 and was finally completed in 1788. Originally the building housed a statue of Saint George including a statue of justice however the statue of justice was destroyed by invading French troops in 1812. Vladimir Lenin had his study and a private apartment on the third floor of the building he used the office between 1918-1922. Later Joseph Stalin used a study including a conference hall housed within the senate. In 1998 the Russian presidential administration was housed within the senate building. Meanwhile the most powerful men in modern Russia entered the building and still had no idea to why they were summoned to an audience with the president, the prime minister had an inkling as to why they had been summoned but kept it to himself. Anatoly hadn't wanted to let the cat out of the bag, not just yet anyway. Earlier in the morning the FSB thoroughly searched the building from top to bottom they were searching for any listening devices. The cleaning staff also had their ID's, identity documents and double checked anyone who wasn't in possession of the correct security pass were immediately turned away from the building. Some Moscow police officers were even sent back to their respective police stations to be replaced by specialist FSB personnel and dog teams who scoured the building searching for any IEDs, Improvised Explosive Devices. The FSB agents deployed Electronic jamming devices to help stop any determined terrorist from electronically or remotely setting off a device from a safe distance away. Eves dropping devices which may have been missed during the searches would be electronically jammed. Outside of the building within the kremlin grounds drones were used to spot anything suspiciously placed in and around the large estate inside the Kremlin grounds. Meanwhile as soon as the delegates arrived the Russian prime minister and the ministers were all electronically frisked for hidden weapons or any recording devices, the electronic security device used on the delegates was very much like walking through an airport security system. One minister remarked to a colleague "the boss must have something very serious on his mind, I don't like the look of this, bringing everyone together like this it normally meant trouble with a big T" As soon as the ministers had been screened they then waited with the prime minister in a much larger hall and they were provided with refreshments, many spoke to each other some of them hadn't seen one another for a good few months and just then seen walking into the hall was the Minister of Defence, General of the Army Vasyli Kuznetsova and the Chief of the General Staff General of the Army Tara Vasiliev, securely fastened to their writs were briefcases the Generals were armed with their military issued pistols. The ministers gathered and stood in silence in the hall they felt the same about why they were summoned because it felt to them something was seriously wrong and no one picked up on the reason to why they were summoned to an audience with the President and they were all unaware of what was about to happen. Both Generals approached the prime minister and they came to a very smart halt in front of him and they saluted him in military precision. All three of the men spoke quietly to one another it was only for a minute or two all the time the others in the hall watched all three from a distance. The smartly dressed Generals soon left the prime minister to get themselves a cup of strong coffee and they both stood well away from the group of ministers. After ten minutes or so the conference room doors were opened by a dark suited man who looked like a typical close protection agent, or a member of the mafia whichever you might prefer. He announced, "gentlemen Mr President will see you now" and with that they all entered a very large conference room and inside the room was extremely plush with many historic paintings adorning the large walls. Before the agent closed the doors behind him he said, "gentlemen you will find your place names on the table please do not swap them over" and with that he proceeded to close the doors behind him and he left the room. Outside of the conference room he sat down on a chair close to the doors. As he sat down he made a quick radio check with his sergeant to ensure his radio earpiece was in working order and after the call he ensured his personal weapon, his SPS, the serdyukov pistol, was sat firmly within its holster it was housed inside his suit jacket. After the checks he felt he could relax a little as he knew he would be bored stupid sat outside of the conference room as it was going to be a very long day. Inside the conference room the dignitaries were chatting between one another, they were still waiting for the president to arrive, suddenly, a door in a corner of the conference room opened and in walked the Russian President. As he approached the large table which was sat in the centre of the room the dignitaries stood up, the president, Anatoly stood by his chair and said "gospoda, pozhaluysta, syad'te. Gentlemen, please sit down. He waited for everyone to sit back down and after they were settled he began to address all those present, "davayte ne budem tseremonitsya, eto ne ofitsial'naya vstrecha, let's not stand on ceremony this is not a formal meeting". With that one or two of the ministers looked at one another some had raised an eyebrow. Was it just possible that it was the way the meeting would pan out, relaxed and informal. Anatoly was about to drop a bombshell to everyone sat inside the splendid and historic room. The venue was very apt, the president knew it was the perfect venue, he had gathered all the ministers to the building for a very historic reason and it was why he called the conference of ministers. His speech would be very apt within the Kremlin because in 1812 during the French had invaded Russia, the invasion was known as the Patriotic War of 1812. The French army entered the very same building where the President, Prime Minister and the ministers were gathered. During World War II the German Army the "Wehrmacht" also invaded Russia and advanced almost eighteen miles to just outside of Moscow and some German Officers could just make out some of the Kremlin's distinctive buildings through their field glasses. A German reconnaissance battalion also found themselves roughly eleven miles away from the Kremlin and within reach of central Moscow, but they had to withdraw because it was due to the fierce resistance put up by the Russian forces who were defending the city. In December 1941 the Russian military eventually and after a struggle began to push the German Army from the area surrounding Moscow and it was eventually the beginning of Russia's efforts to push back the German invasion from Russian soil. It was with this background of Russian history in mind Anatoly called for the meeting to be held in the Kremlin. He stood up and flipped through a folder that was laying on the large conference table in front of him. He quickly covered the history of the other countries who over the years had invaded Russia including countries who during the Soviet Union cold war periods formed part of the then Russian "empire". After a short and a very brief history lesson he then invited the two generals to brief the ministers on the current state of the modern Russian armed forces and the readiness of the military to either thwart an invasion of Russia by NATO forces and to brief those in the room on how best placed the Russian military were in carrying out a Russian invasion of Europe. When the Russian President mentioned "invading Europe" the delegates could not help but repeat the words invasion. Anatoly brought the meeting to order "dzhentl'men tsitiruyet, gentlemen quite". "istoriya na nashey storone, history is on our side". The president's words resonated around the room and once the ministers calmed down there was an eerie silence within the room. To some who were sat at the table his words sounded ominous and very threatening. Anatoly invited the Minister of Defence, General of the Army Vasyli Kuzetsovo to start his briefing by now the General uncoupled the briefcase from around his wrist and he began to open the secure briefcase case contained inside there were various maps and a Top-Secret briefing pack. Within the conference room there was

Credit

a projection room it was where the Chief of the General Staff General Tara Vasiliev had quickly moved to, the contents of the briefing were highly classified, and it was extremely politically sensitive, to say the least, for just any old soldier to operate the slide projector and to then listen to the top secret briefing hence why a General was currently sat inside the projector room and clicking through the various slides during the briefing. On a large screen inside the projection room appeared a slide of a map of Western Europe including the United Kingdom. General Kuznetsova began to read from the briefing pack and he began by formally addressing the group "Mr President and gentlemen as you can see from the map, a map you are all very familiar with because it is the map of Europe, gentlemen the time is just right for Russia to expand militarily into western Europe it is also possible to invade the United Kingdom, it would be further than the Nazis ventured during the second world war". Within the room was an audible and nervous shuffling from many of the delegates and who were by now sitting uncomfortably around the table. He allowed them a few minutes to settle back down again and to allow them to take in what had been said, the delegates knew that the President would have known what the content of the briefing would contain as it had his hands all over it, as there was no way on earth two Generals would have dreamt of such an audacious idea that of invading Europe without having the Presidents knowledge. He went on to elaborate on what he meant "The UK has never been militarily naked because of its own government because nearly every part of its military infrastructure has been reduced in size to numbers not seen since before the first world war and its own government has all but mothed balled its nuclear submarine fleet deterrent" the general, thought it was time once again to just pause a little to allow the delegates to take in the next slide it was a slide showing

116

the strength of Britain's military forces and its equipment the figures on the graph looked very dire indeed he carried on with the briefing "Europe at this precise moment in time is fighting one another and NATO has been weakened all due to the UK having left the alliance, The President has invested heavily in our own armed forces and for which I can vouch for, the whole nation is grateful for his foresight". Another slide appeared, it showed the current deployment of NATO forces some of which were stationed within some of the old soviet union's satellite states. The General went on to explain of his concerns and he began by pointing out, France was a country with its own independent nuclear capability even though France was part of NATO, its independent nuclear capability was totally independent from NATO, it was controlled by France's military and its deployment was ultimately authorised by the President of France. It has a very well trained and highly disciplined standing Army. Germany did not possess a Nuclear capability, but what it did have was a professional and a well-trained Army with a fully mechanised capability. Germany's military possessed a high proportion of anti-tank and tank destroying equipment and their main battle tank, MBT, was the vastly superior Leopard 2 tank. There were a couple of other European countries who also operated the Leopard 2 MBT, Main Battle Tank. Over the years the British Army had withdrawn from what was West Germany by now all British forces had returned to military bases in Britain, once in Britain the current British government went about almost destroying the Army and its capability to operate as an effect fighting force and so was its capability of ever deploying an Army in any future war or conflict it would be extremely difficult to put together a Corps the size of which is approximately fifty thousand men including the equipment to become an effective fighting force. During the same briefing the General also pointed out he

personally thought it was a disgrace of how a country such as
Great Britain could allow so many of its famous Regiments be
disbanded. In summing up his briefing he concluded that a
successful invasion of such a vast land mass, as Europe was a big
step for Russia and speed was of the essence once deployed to
War. He also admitted it would take roughly a year to build up
the manpower including the equipment that was needed to
successfully win a lightening war. One of his reasons for such a
long time to build up manpower and the equipment to support an
invasion of Europe was if Russian forces were to be successful
and able to defeat so many European country's armies. The
Russian Army would have to station some troops on the ground
within the conquered areas and the defeated countries troops
would have to help run the overrun countries and the state
apparatus alongside the civilian police. When the General
finished the briefing, the president tanked him, it was then the
President invited both Generals to leave the conference room.
Once they left the room the Prime minister spoke "gentlemen
now you have it!!" Most of the minister's present were utterly
astonish and were so dumfounded about what they just heard.
Anatoly stood up from his chair and spoke "I know it is a lot to
take in, but I am hoping I will not have any dissenters? to my
plans obviously there is so much more detail to my plan of action,
the ministers knew what their fate would be if they dissented,
my first plan is to use North Korea as a distraction and then to
soften up the British Prime minister the country is almost
bankrupt, I am going to offer his government lots of money to
base Russian aircraft and our warships in Britain's ports NATO is
weak without Britain within its ranks".
The Russian Prime Minister Vladimir Sokolov informed the
delegates that in a few weeks they would each receive a briefing
pack with instructions for what their departments and areas of

government would be responsible for they would all have certain equipment quotes to produce for example munitions, fighting vehicles, food for the troops etc. To some of the ministers sitting in the room it was pure madness a nightmare waiting to happen. Not many thoughts there was any need to invade the west, but it seemed to evolve around more land for instance the Baltic states were always viewed by the Russians as being part of a greater Russia it was much the same with Poland and other European countries, Russia had always viewed them as Russian, and the Ukraine Russians were in recent years involved in a proxy war with The Ukraine. Russia also laid claims on large swathes of land as far away south as Tajikistan. Many of the former Soviet states were awaiting confirmation of their current applications to join the European Union some were also in the throes of forging alliances with NATO and it was all too much for Russia. It was yet another reason why the President wanted to invade western Europe as he knew full well if he went through with his plans he would have to defeat NATO and quickly before America could launch a response because the Russians hoped to be at that the coast of France and if the US did decide to use its nuclear weapons or battlefield tactical nuclear weapons they would end up possibly killing millions of innocent European civilians. Anatoly knew that his forces would have to be very quick to overrun the western European countries he knew America would not launch nuclear tactical battlefield weapons he knew America could not justify so many innocent casualties. The Russian military were always worried about America and France because of the country's nuclear capabilities. Even more so with a president in the US who did not have any qualms carrying out the unexpected, whatever it was. It would take the Generals in Russia many months to work out a fool proof strategy of attack. They hoped the politicians could bluff the west and to lull their governments into a false sense of security. The generals had known from history that Germany was ideal tank country as it proved during world war two when Russia invaded Germany during the defeat of Adolf Hitler's Military. But during the invasion pushing the German out of Russia they soon found that the Germans were excellent at the art of anti-tank ambushes hence why Russia lost so many tanks and manpower during this phase of the war and the Russian Generals were aware of the attrition of equipment and manpower. If they wanted to fight a conventional war the act of war it would have to be at the right time and quickly executed on Russia's terms when the country was ready. But if Battle Field Tactical Nuclear weapons were used it would be a totally different kettle of fish. Many a Russian citizen did not want a war they were so used to peace and many younger people had never known Russia being at war be it World War two or the Cold War. Meanwhile in America the President called an urgent meeting regarding what he could see an alarming situation in Britain he was concerned about both the political and the alarming military situation. He demanded his Chief of Staff of the US Army Bob Sparks and the Secretary of Défense Mark Wiseman be there and he made a call to the vice president Michael Smit and he briefed him about the meeting and confirmed he would attend, the president told Michael to round up the Head of American Homeland Security, Labor and the Treasury and bring them with him. It was to be a Top Secret, American eyes-only meeting. No one was to know about the agenda until everyone was sat around the conference table. If anyone leaked anything he told him they would be sacked immediately. At the same time the world was in such turmoil and no government wanted to unnecessary panic their own citizens. There was a much greater threat from terrorist organisations and any sleeper cells, none of the European government knew of

Russia's plans this was yet another threat from Russia by assisting terrorist groups to hit most of the European cities before any full frontal Russian attack on the west? It would help Russia shine the spotlight away from their plans for any invasion. Allied security services would be distracted by the concerted attacks by terrorist groups, funded by Russia. The director of the FSB passed a classified document to the Russian Prime minister requesting that the FSB should close all social media sites in the country and limit the Russian public to the world wide web. He refused the directors request because he thought by closing and denying Russian citizens access would alert the Americans something was afoot and so it was better to leave things as they were but for the FSB to continue the monitoring of all web networks. One of the more secret kremlin departments began to flood North Korea with misinformation. The Russian ambassador to North Korea had been informed that recently North Korea opened diplomatic access to South Korea including America, The Russian Ambassador delivered misinformation to his counterpart in the capital Pyongyang. A spy in the North Korean government got wind of some Russian documents and copied the documents and he sent them to the Chinese Secret Service the Ministry of State Security, MSS, who then forwarded the documents to the Ministry of Défense. The Minister of Défense himself thought when he had read the documents wondered why the Russians were circulating fake news, unless there was something more sinister going on in the background. He sat thinking to himself "is this just a ploy to deflect something else that is going on with the Russians"? Surprisingly the Chinese tipped off the American Ambassador to China. This was something the Russians did not factor into their war plans it was the human element and things do not always do what is expected of them. They wanted North Korea to distract the Americans from their own deception in the Sea of Japan and it was a deliberate ploy for America to divert so more of their forces to Japan and the Korean peninsula. As far as the Russians were concerned the deception had worked. The Americans also requested the Chinese to allay North Korea's fears and to get the North Koreans to go along with the Russian deception. China agreed but they wanted the Americans to calm the South Koreans fears and not to let them fall into the Russian deception trap. The countries in the region agreed and went along with the deception. In Moscow things in the Korean and Chinese area of influence was going exactly to plan, or so they thought. They had no idea of what was happening in the region or how closely China and America were working together on the diplomatic front. America took the UK out of the intelligence sharing loop as they couldn't trust the British any more. The British government were more concerned about where they were going to get some more investment from. The Russian proposition was looking the most favourable. The Americans kept its Embassy in London fully manned as they hadn't broken off all diplomatic contact with the British even though the embargo was crippling the country. The mole within No 10 Downing street was very active. It was soon time for the Central Intelligence Agency, CIA the American overseas Intelligence agency to make direct contact with the mole but they were monitoring the mole very closely to confirm the information he or she was providing to see if it was genuine or not. Over time it was confirmed the information provided was indeed genuine. The CIA and the American intelligence services wanted far more specific information and quickly, for instance what were China and Russia offering the British Prime Minister for the use of the country's military bases.

Chapter 7 – Monitoring the People

The Chinese were surprisingly open about their interest in the UK they indicated to the Americans the apparent willingness of the British government to allow China the use of their many military airbases and their ports for the right amount of money and to the highest bidder. The Americans correctly concluded if the Chinese have been offered the use of the British bases it was more than likely that the Russians were involved in a bidding war. The Chinese Ambassador to Washington took the extraordinary step of briefing the American Défense Secretary everything the Chinese had known about the UK offer and the amount of money the British government also wanted for the use of their military bases. The Ambassador mentioned the General Secretary of the Communist Party of China who is also the President and head of state had wanted to do more than the sharing of intelligence with the Americans. There was a very high probability Russia was up to something because the Russians dearly wanted to obtain a foot hold on the Island of Great Britain. The American Défense Secretary sat up and he took more notice when the Chinese Ambassador took the unusual step of being open and candid when she mentioned the Chinese government was open to further intelligence and for the start of military cooperation between China and America. What she told the Americans had obviously been sanctioned by the communist party in Beijing. When the meeting was over with the pair shook hands in what seemed like a genuine hand of friendship. As soon as the Ambassador left the office the Défense Secretary sat his chair he was deep in thought regarding what just happened in his office. It was as though the Chinese were warning America of something which hadn't yet happened, not yet anyway? He was an historian and the meeting had been just like history repeating itself. He thought about the time leading up to the Japanese bombing of Pearl Harbour in December 1941. He immediately contacted the President's office and he requested an audience with the President. The following morning the Defence Secretary found himself sat inside the oval office along with the President. He briefed the President; on what the Chinese Ambassador to the US had said to him the previous day the President was extremely alarmed at what the Défense Secretary had to say so much, so, he called for a security meeting for the following day. In the Presidents mind there was too many coincidences and because of what was happening on the world stage all of which, could be pointed directly at the feet of the Russians. Alarm bells were sounding within corridors of power in Washington, long before the Défense Secretary's briefing, and it seemed to stem from the political and military situation within the UK. The Americans fully understood why Chinas diplomats were offering Intelligence information, some of which the Americans had already gathered themselves regarding Russia's true intentions. The Americans knew the Chinese wanted to deflect from their own intentions within the South China seas more so their military expansion within the area. America had a very large Naval and Marine presence in Japan also in the Philippines and they would remain in the area as it would have been so easy to believe everything that China was saying and to move American military forces from the region. What worried the American administration the most about Europe and it was the United Kingdom the American food embargo it was still in place and the President knew it was hurting the British people and believe it or not it hurt him deeply, knowing what it was doing to the country, but he felt it had to be done, he wasn't worried about the British government because he blamed them wholeheartedly for the current situation that the British people found themselves in. The President formulated a plan in his head it certainly did not include Britain's government. Americas best academic minds from around the country all got their heads together and they informed the president, they could not see the current UK government remaining in power for much longer. However, the "think" tank had no idea of what the President had recently found out about what China and Russia were offering the British government for the use of the country's military bases and more shocking was the Chines nor the Russians military could be based within the UK. The President knew full well he would have to move quickly as time was fast running out. He needed to catch the UK off guard. Meanwhile the British opposition parties were at long last, getting their act together and were now beginning to formulate a plan to topple the sitting government from power and it would have to be done democratically, no coup. Many voters within the country were starting to find their voice and were now voicing their anger at what the government were doing, and Britain was on the brink of considering the dark abys. Some of the government's own policies and they were policies brought before parliament for the very first time they were voted down by the opposition coalition party, it was a start and in it was in the right direction, at last there was a viable opposition within the houses of parliament. One bill failed to pass in the house and it was a bill to allow the government to hire military bases to the highest bidder be it China or Russia, the reason for the bill was to bring, the much-needed funds, into the treasury coffers the Russians recently added it was also willing to pay part of the bill with grain and it was part of Russia's surplus harvest. The bill would have to come back to the house with various tweaks, and still the Prime

Minister was still hell bent on getting the bill past, through parliament and quickly. During the vote the opposition called for a three-line whip, which meant every opposition MP would have to turn up and to vote no matter what. Some MPs were ill and at home but none the less they were determined to attend the house of commons to vote and some MP's were wheeled into the voting chamber of the house of Parliament and others flew back to the UK having curtailed their holidays the opposition successfully rejected the governments, bill. The skulduggery being spun well away from the glare of the press and the people of the country, it was the dark side of politics, the events behind the scenes could have so easily brought the country to the brink of war. Many of the veterans were still communicating via social media and had no idea of what was going on all around them and of course it wasn't their place to know. They were still disillusioned with how their own politicians were ruling their respective countries. In London George could not believe the country's opposition parties still hadn't got their acts together to bring down the government, as he often said it was a "bloody disgrace". All because of the opposition party's inability to act as a meaningful opposition to the governments hair brained policy's it meant the government still held onto a majority in parliament and it enabled them to keep an iron grip on the country. Unknown to George it was all going to change in Parliament and there was now a viable opposition coalition and him being a military type of person, he was very concerned about the way the military over the past two years were severely reduced in size. After he been on one of his "benders" at his local pub he was sat in his bedsit he only just about managed to log onto his favourite social media site. Where he mistakenly fired off a tirade of abuse aimed at the British Prime minister and his government and after a short while George promptly fell asleep in a drunken stupor, when he eventually managed to rouse himself in the early hours of the following morning he could see his laptop was still switched on and he managed to open one eye and then the other one and at first thought that he dropped the laptop during the night and he may have broken the screen. Luckily it wasn't damaged, and he could see he was still logged onto the social media site as he hadn't logged out the previous evening, because he was so drunk. As he wiped his eyes to remove the congealed sleep from around his eyes he noticed he received many messages most where regarding his recent rant online. There were some messages from other ex British military veterans they all agreed with what he posted during his drunken state last night. But there was a mystery message and it made him sit up and take notice and when he looked at it more closely the message warned him to be very careful about what he wished for, as it may come true. George was intrigued by the message, but not scared in any way, he could see it was sent by a member of the group and he knew by being a member of the group did not prove in anyway, who the person really was, it could be a nutter for all he knew. He replied to the message and left it at that. Later, the same morning he looked for a reply but there wasn't one, and so after a day or and so he left it as that it could have been sent by another veteran who also had been on a bender. It nonetheless played somewhat on his mind and George thought to himself "who the bloody hell was it who sent me that bloody message, very spooky". Elsewhere in London an American CIA, Central Intelligence Agency operative had joined the veteran's social media site and he began to monitor the other members messages. Immediately Ivor from Russia his messages caught the agents eye only because Ivor's messages were a little too strong for them not to have been picked up by the Russian FSB and he was very curious as to why he seemed to have got away with his comments and his rants against the Russian President. The CIA agent adopted the pseudonym name Frank, living in New York and served in Afghanistan as a US Marine, he most probably did serve out there that much was more than likely true, the stage was now set. At the same time as the French had welcomed the British Prime Minister for having opened the British borders to allow many thousands of immigrants and refugees to freely enter the UK as many thousands had been previously housed at the many refugee camps scattered around many French ports and of course central Paris. After a couple of years Britain soon found itself unable to cope with the huge influx of people entering the country at the same time it also unwittingly allowed many terrorists to also gain entry to the country. At the same time some sleeper cells were waiting until enough weapons, ammunition and high-quality military bomb making material, arrived in the country to enable them carry out acts of terror, the material was being gathered for the right time to carry out many terrorist atrocities. These people weren't on any of the Intelligence services database or on the radar and it meant for now the terrorists hadn't been tracked or monitored, they were for now free to roam the country unhindered. The terrorist Central coordinating cell had a terrorist sympathiser working within the Metropolitan police headquarters, in London, surprisingly he managed to obtain access to the anti-terrorist branch's computer network and he was drip feeding the coordinator of a terrorist group and he supplied him with very high grade and confidential anti-terrorist information and of course it was beneficial to the group. The smaller terrorist cells did not know about one another enabling security to be tight. The mole within the Met police had security clearance to work within the Metropolitan police Headquarters, recently he was chatting to other organisations in and around the middle east and he was soon "turned" and he sympathised with their cause he wanted to help in any way to cause as much mayhem in London. The terrorists who were smuggled into the UK were of a mixture of many different cultures and nations some came from, the Middle East, Africa, the Sub Continent, Europe and Britain. All of them had witnessed and fought in many far-flung countries as mercenaries but they hadn't been fighting on the side of good. They all had one thing in common and it was a deep hatred towards Britain and its people. As soon as Britain opened its borders and without having carried out any form of checks on those who were flowing into the country in their droves it was just the opportunity the terrorists dreamed of. It was such a great opportunity to smuggle terrorists into the United Kingdom and without the fear of being stopped. The central terrorist cell soon moved weapons, ammunition and explosives to some safe houses and at the various drop off points throughout the country with sympathisers who believed in their cause. The coordinators would never get their hands dirty by showing any of those operating inside the terror cells the coordinators could never show the others what they looked like and contact was always through third parties everything that was needed by the terrorists was always paid for in cash only. The smuggled weapons were now confirmed as being safely stashed and ready for collection when the time was right. They would always use someone they codenamed the "Armourer" he never got to see anyone within the coordinating cell he only liaised with the owners of the safe houses. The Prime Minister Julien Jones soon realised it was time for the country to close the open borders. He realised along with the Americans and his government by submitted the country to a crippling food embargo and having almost brought the country to the verge of bankruptcy and recently the population of the UK was by now up in arms regarding high taxes, lack of food and the rationing of certain foods and of course at the huge influx of migrants swamping and overwhelming the nations, meagre resources, it was the common-sense thing to do before it was far too late to do anything to reverse things. Most people in the country did agree with migration but only drip-fed migration as to not overburden the country's infrastructure and to integrate those who were lucky enough to be accepted into the mainstream refuge system. But to have opened the flood gates because it was the PM's moral crusade it hadn't worked. In Moscow the Russian president was ready to offer the British a much-needed cash lifeline, it would enable the Russians to rent in the knowledge they would have unfettered access to the many British military bases. The Russian President offered the Prime Minister a meeting in Kaliningrad the capital of the Russian province of the same name. The province is situated between Poland and Lithuania on the Baltic coast. The city was largely rebuilt post World War II because the Russians had pulverised the former German city, it was almost levelled to the ground.

The Russian President wanted to offer Britain a very handsome amount of money for his military to be able to stage through Britain? The mole at No 10 Downing Street had managed to get sight of the Russian invite to Kaliningrad and she managed to safely send a copy of the invite to her contact in the Défense Department in America who immediately sent the report to the American Défense Secretary who in turn informed President Zoola of its contents. To say it was a shock to him was an understatement as he knew he would have to act and very quickly bearing in mind he hadn't spoken to the Prime Minister since he enforced Americas food embargo almost eighteen months ago and much had passed under the bridge since then. The President picked up one of the many telephones on his desk and asked to be directly connected to the British Prime Minister's office. It was 8 am Washington time and 4 pm in the UK. The Prime Minister Julien Jones despised the American President Mark Zoola the feeling was mutual but on this occasion the call was more courteous "Mr President what can I do for you, it is a pleasure to speak to you" The President did not beat about the bush and said, "I know the UK has monetary problems and now I hear you are offering the use of your military facilities to China and Russia?" At first the Prime Minister was lost for words and initially he did not know what to say in reply all he could say was "yes we are" the president knew he had some space to diplomatically manoeuvre regarding the UK's problems and offered the Prime Minister a financial loan for the Americans to rent the British bases at a very fair rate it was more money than the Chinese and Russians had offered the British. The Prime Minister asked the President if he could find his way to end the food blockade, but the President emphatically replied "no". The Prime Minister then requested could he get back to him regarding the American President's very reasonable financial offer for the use of the UK's military bases. The President replied, "you have a week and if I hear nothing in that time then the deal will be off the table" he slammed the phone down on the Prime Minister, Julien didn't have time to reply. In his office the Prime Minister was smiling he naively thought "good there is now a bidding war between America, China and Russia, little did he know. He was very annoyed, only because the president would not lift the food embargo as he could have used the success of lifting the embargo to his own benefit, as there was to be a general election the following year. At that precise moment in time he knew his government would not be re-elected for a second term. But there could have been more of a chance of winning the next general election if he could just get the food embargo lifted. Some people would have said pigs might fly. Meanwhile the American President was hedging his bets he desperately wanted to "scare" off the Chinese and the Russians from the idea of using the British military bases and he wanted to somehow prevent them from using the bases without ever firing a shot in anger. He began by contacting some of the NATO's heads of state and he concentrated on Canada, Denmark, France, Germany and Norway because he wanted each of them to form a naval blockade around the coast of the UK and to put even more pressure on the British government. Luckily every head of state agreed to provide Warships and submarines to aid in the US blockade of the UK, it was a huge gamble. Within a week the United Kingdom soon found itself surrounded by many NATO warships they were stationed just off the UK and in International waters. Unknown to NATO the action had put the Russians noses out of joint. No one apart from the Russians were aware of why they were so keen on using the British bases and the proposed invasion of western Europe. The Commander in Chief of the Russian Navy recently submitted a report to the Minister for Defence pointing out the latest and sudden build-up of NATOs Naval warships around the coast of the United Kingdom. Several of France's nuclear submarine fleet had been supplemented by some of Americas nuclear submarines and they were patrolling the international waters surrounding the Island of Great Britain. It was a deliberate ploy by NATO more so America, to make the Russians aware of the submarines presence. The submarines were supported by a surface fleet and by now there was a substantial naval force surrounding the British Isles. Unknown to anyone including NATO and the Russians, America had recently deployed one of its Nuclear-powered aircraft carriers and it was

132

heading at full steam toward British waters. The Chinese government suddenly contacted the British government to inform the Prime Minister that the deal to pay for the use of the British military bases was off the table as it wasn't viable any more due to the deployment of so much military hardware just off the coast of Britain. Britain had suddenly become a very hot potato, too hot to handle. The Russian President had once again called upon his ministers and his military top brass it was only then he took the decision to place the invasion of western Europe on hold there was far too much heat being generated in and around Britain, NATO having deploying warships in international waters all around the coast of Britain and it was too much of a risk for the Russian forces to invade Europe, it proved to the Russians NATO could still muster large forces in a very short period of time, something the Russians did not expect. Both France and Germany had deployed their country's military on a war footing. In the South China seas Japan was placed on heightened alert and the Philippines military were also placed on a war footing it was all due to China's expansion plans in around the International seas around the Philippines. The Russian President Anatoly thought his plans to invade western Europe was far too much of a risk to the Russian state. A day after his decision to climb down from starting World War III a report landed on his desk it pointed out an American aircraft carrier had recently arrived off the coast of Great Britain. All he could do was to contact the British Prime Minister Julien Jones and to inform him officially that he would reluctantly have to pull out of any deal to use the UK's military bases. The mole working within No. 10 Downing Street got to hear about the Prime Minister and the Russian Presidents recent telephone call and she informed the Americans about the Chinese and the Russia's decision to finally withdrawal from any deal regarding the use of military bases within the UK the American President was by now primed for his next plan of action. The British Prime Minister had totally misjudged the US President, he was far more astute than Julien ever gave him credit for, more by luck or bad luck, who will ever know? Meanwhile in a non-descript looking semidetached house in the midlands a man was hunched over a laptop, the light from the screen highlighting his face in the darkness, he was surfing on the dark web and messaging someone based in the middle east. The message was short and very much to the point. He was sat waiting for a reply from the contact he soon received a reply he then replied to the message, "everything is in place" a reply to his message came back and it was once very short "go" and the link was suddenly cut off by the man in the middle east. The man sat inside a house, in the UK, was smiling. Sat on a coffee table in the living room were ten different mobile phones they were all pay as you go phones. He had been waiting for this day for almost a year. It took such a long time for the plan to come together and to organise and put everything into place for it to work, hence the recent contact to the man in the middle east. The man was still sat in his living room looking at the phones, he was just a small cog in a much larger machine. He had no idea of the bigger picture nor who the man in the middle east was. The man in the UK was known as Awamiri and he hated the British people because as a child he was told many stories about the horrific aftermath after the British granted independence to India and Pakistan after so many years of colonial rule. His grandfather left Pakistan as a young boy to settle in Britain together with his mother and father. Awamiri worked in IT with an IT company it was based in Birmingham. To many of his work colleagues he was a bit of an IT geek and he would keep himself to himself. Beneath the veneer of normality, he was a very angry man who went on to despise western society more so the British. And so, he eventually turned to vent his anger on the internet on the "dark web". It was whilst he was on the dark web he was eventually recruited by the "controller" with so much ease and he soon managed to persuade Awamiri to assist in avenging the people of the middle east for the west taking part in the many wars within the region, by helping to carry out terrorist acts in the UK he became a willing recruit. The "controller" and other people from terrorist organisations would never have to get their hands dirty they always used willing foot soldiers who were willingly carry out their dirty work without themselves having to get involved or be seen executing their warped plans to kill so many innocent people. Awamiri had previously received eleven, pay as you go mobile phones by courier he was given instructions to hide the phones sent by the "controller" and he was briefed to let the ten two-man terrorist teams who were also recruited to carry out the next terrorist atrocities in the UK to wait for further instructions. Each team was to be sent a pay as you go phone by Awamiri as it was Awamiri who held all of the other cells contact numbers each team was informed in a note sent with the phones, they were to await instructions as to where and when they were to pick up their allocated weapons, ammunition and the bomb making equipment   As soon as the cells received their instructions they were to destroy the phones and the SIM cards and both items were to be destroyed separately and under no circumstances were they to be destroyed together. The controller would soon provide instructions to each cell the instructions will provide the details of the nominated targets each team would attack, via the dark web. Because of the use of hire vans by previous terrorist groups to carry out other terrorist atrocities.

Monitoring the People

The teams were going to have to walk or travel by bus or rail to get to their targets. All twenty terrorists were to prepare mentally and religiously for the upcoming missions they were all aware during the attacks they could all be killed. Some of the men and the women knew full well that they might not be returning from their "missions" and they knew that they were going to murder innocent people just going about their ordinary business not doing any harm to anyone. The "controller" was aware of the current British government's policy regarding the countries own armed forces and he knew all about the significant cut backs to the British armed forces including its inability to operate as a deterrent to attacks inside the UK, he was very pleased to note the government's policy of cutting back on the policing budget. He realised the capital was heavily policed and as such he needed to come up with a unique plan of action, something the police would not expect. He also studied the areas he had identified to be "hit" and he meticulously planned the terrorist attack over a long time. His intelligence on the ground was excellent and much up to date. Because of Britain's borders having recently been flung wide open without any checks the "controller" was able to move some very experienced and battle hardened, terrorists into the UK. He had the terrorist sympathiser working close to the Metropolitan police to help with police intelligence the information helped with the planning of the upcoming terrorist operation. Those who were hiding the terrorist's arms caches were recently warned to expect various strangers to contact them and within the month, they were collecting the stash of munitions and whoever it was contacting them, at the safe houses, would have a code word, at some stage they would be sent a secret code to allow the "visitors" to collect the arms cache's. The controller finally picked the area's where the terrorist cells were to attack and to cause as much mayhem within the shortest possible time. The "controller" was extremely smart he had carried out his homework with precision he knew the police could not be everywhere certainly not in the areas he was going to deploy the terrorist cells to, carrying out a terrorist in the selected areas would cause maximum alarm and if the police caught or stopped one cell there would be 7 other cells all in different parts of the country who would simultaneously carry out many acts of terrorism. At the same time Britain's security services were distracted by other matters such as an attack by cyber terrorists who were trying to attack the country's infrastructure and its military computer systems Britain still had NATO warships standing off the British coast. The government were inflicting so much hardship on the people of Britain and it lay at the door of the government. Food was still being rationed and America hadn't lifted the food embargo on the country. The Prime Ministers gamble of generating extra money by "renting" Britons military bases to three, one being America, foreign powers by now had sensationally back fired. The Americans by now had also pulled out of the negotiations for the use of the British bases. The country was slowly grinding to a halt by now food was in such short supply personal taxes rose to astronomical levels. The people were beginning to voice their dissent at both the government. The opposition finally got their act together and were now defeating the government when it came to the vote on the various desperate policies brought before the house of parliament. The Prime Minister was still sticking to his ludicrous principles and Marxist policies very much to the detriment of the people he was meant to be serving. His government was still funding terrorist organisations using the Foreign Overseas Aid Budget. There were many calls in Parliament for the Aid handed out to these organisations to be stopped immediately. Things were not going the governments way anymore and it may have taken a long time for the opposition to get their act together, but they finally became a viable opposition, the government weren't getting things their own way, any more. The American President understood the British Government was beginning to sink in their filthy viper's nest, it was about time. He was so annoyed at the lack of action by the opposition parties and he felt they were all inept especially after he had done so much to bring down the current British government. The US Défense Secretary requested the President to contact the NATO Secretary General to cease the naval blockade of the UK, the President spoke "no not just yet I want to keep the squeeze on the British government". Meanwhile the" spy" working in the Metropolitan Police Headquarters in London somehow managed to get his hands on a document sent by the Home Office Minister and it was addressed to the Metropolitan Police Commissioner, the "spy" found the letter on an email attachment the letter was attached in error. He managed to save the letter to his hard drive. When he tried to look for the original email to check who had sent the letter the email including the attachment was deleted, obviously it had been sent in error. He sent the letter to his cloud account and then he deleted it from his PC's hard drive. That evening at home he sat reading the letter and was from the Home Office Minister himself he was demanding the Commissioner to make even more cost saving cuts to the Mets police's budget without harming the anti-terrorist policing budget and he warned the commissioner if she made any cuts to the anti-terrorist budget, the opposition and the public would not allow the cuts to go ahead. After having reading, the letter the "spy" contacted the "controller" via the dark web and he sent the Home Officer Minister's letter to the "Controller". The "controller" now had first hand, knowledge regarding the state of the Met police force and the kind of pressure the Police Commissioner was put under by politicians. The Prime Minister called for a meeting of his inner cabinet at Number 10 Downing Street. There was much on the agenda for the meeting and the first two items on the agenda was the continuation of the Americans food embargo and NATO's continued Naval blockade of the UK. Julien duly briefed the cabinet as he thought the two blockades, the American food, and NATO Naval blockade, could continue for many months to come. His other item was the possible future unrest of the British people there was a worry that people could riot due to the food crises. He asked the Minister for Defence and the Home secretary if the Military and the Police could enforce Martial Law if it came to it? it would mean the suspension of normal law and a military government running taking control of the country. Both ministers replied in unison "no". The Defence Minister went on to say, "Julien the Military has recently been cut to the bone, but I suppose we could enforce martial law for the maximum of a number of weeks but no more". The Home secretary spoke up "Julien perhaps for a week or two but no longer". Julien was then briefed by the Home Secretary who by now was joined by the heads of MI5, MI6 including the head of GCHQ, the Government Communications Headquarters. All three went on to brief the Prime Minister and his ministers regarding the communications traffic on the internet including the dark web? The head of MI6 had "contacts" within the middle east who had recently confirmed something big was going to happen in the UK, but the "contacts" did not know exactly where or when or what form it would take. The PM over the past couple of years had many a run in with the three security agencies and it was due to his decision to the opening of the country to untethered immigration. The Home Secretary was suddenly on the side of three heads of UK security, perhaps he could visualize his future position if there was a spectacular terrorist situation, in the past he looked upon all three security services with suspicion. He now suddenly, he did not wish to be seen when looking back on history the then home secretary who neglected his duty to the people of the UK. Julien noted the Home Secretary's concerns. The Home Secretary's conclusion was to close and immediately the UK borders. He wanted the security services to carry on with their Stirling work and for the government to cease cutting back on the security forces before it was too late. The Prime Minister said he would have to seriously think about closing of the country's borders. With that he concluded the meeting. Back in the midlands Awamiri received a call on his pay as you go mobile and the call was from the "controller" he only said one word "go". At the end of the call all Awamiri could do was to place the phone on top of the coffee table and stared at the mobile. The previous day he received a letter delivered by courier inside the envelope was an A5 piece of paper with numbers listed one to ten and next to each number were a set of map coordinates. He was still shaking five minutes after having received the call. After a few minutes he stopped shaking and took out the piece of paper from within his wallet containing the ten mobile phone numbers he started to phone each mobile phone number and the person who answered the phone he gave them a map reference and after twenty minutes he finished calling the ten terrorist cells. After the calls he walked into the garden and piled garden rubbish into an incinerator and then poured petrol over the piece of paper containing the contact numbers, he also had some other items he did not to fall into the hands of the police, things such as the SIM card from the "spare" mobile and he set fire to the whole lot. It was bin day and for some reason he dropped the spare backup mobile into the rubbish bin. He checked, that he couldn't see the phone inside the bin and so he was finally satisfied no one else could see the phone. He then concentrated on destroying the SIM card still burning away in the fire inside the back garden and he poured yet more petrol over the card. Suddenly he saw a bin lorry arrive in the street and he quickly moved the bin into the street. He walked into the house and he kept an eye on the bin lorry from the safety of his living room. The truck soon pulled up outside of his house. One of the bin men opened the lid of the bin and Awamiri heard one of the bin men shout, "hey Bob look at this" Awamiri thought "fuck me they have found the phone," he noticed his bin being loaded into the bin lorry it spewed its load into the belly of the lorry. After the bin had been emptied it was placed outside of his house. As soon as the lorry drove out of the street he moved the bin inside of the house and straight in to the garden and he checked to see if the bin was empty. He looked at the bonfire and he could see by now there were only the embers of the fire remaining the SIM card had been incinerated. He raked through the fire and he couldn't see any remains of the card. Once satisfied he left the house and paid the rent and his council tax up front for two months in advance. Then he travelled to London to visit relatives meanwhile a member of one of the two-man terrorist cell visited their nominated safe houses during the previous evening to collect his cells allocated weaponry. Each cell disposed of the issued mobiles and accordingly destroyed the SIM cards and most of them burnt the SIM cards, two of the cells used acid on the SIM cards. Meanwhile at GCHQ the operator who was monitoring certain mobile phones emailed his report to his desk manager he pointed out in the report several mobile phones on the list of suspicious mobiles had recently ceased to operate and he also noted the type of inactivity, in the past, having been monitored the phones often turned out to belong to active terrorist groups who went on to blow themselves up in various terrorist attacks on London. The desk officer was aware of just how good his operator was and as such he immediately sent the report to his superior operations officer. His boss phoned the desk officer and told him of what he thought about the lack of use regarding the mobiles and he was also suspicious at the inactivity. The desk officer backed the operators concerns. His boss took the report with and the teams concerns to the head of GCHQ. The head asked the desk officer to sit down "George what do you think "George replied "well sir my operator has noticed over the months the voice traffic between the eleven mobiles within the UK and the one in the middle east. There hadn't been much traffic recently and then all of sudden all twelve phones have suddenly gone off line". "OK George leave it with me and thanks". The head contacted the Home Secretary directly on a secure telephone line. He passed on his concerns to the Home Secretary and he was very concerned and so he called an urgent meeting with the heads of MI5, MI6 and the Metropolitan Police Commissioner. He began to explain to those gathered at the meeting about the concerns raised by the head of GCHQ. He went on to ask if the three heads were as concerned as GCHQ were? All three had no intelligence to go on but the head of MI5 spoke first "well if it is a group of terrorists we could be looking for at least nine to ten terrorists who are on the lose within the UK it is our worst nightmare". The terrorist cells were sitting tight at their allocated safe houses and all of them were trained in the middle east and had undertaken map reading skills and memorised the grid references given to them by Awamiri all of those in the cells knew the numbers were grid references and learnt them back to front and upside down, they did not need anything more to go on. Each team were kept apart and were never in contact with one another, so if caught they only knew member of their own cell and no one could link any of the other cells to one another. Each team were given their target, and, in the safe houses they had access to the internet and were able to use the map references to identify their targets. The scene was now set. They all knew the day on which they were to attack their selected targets and they were not to deviate from the date or the time it was imperative they hit their targets at roughly the same time to ensure maximum impact. Meanwhile in London George was sat in his bedsit waiting for his sister to arrive she was due to take him to her house in the countryside for a short break.

At first, he was very reluctant to go because he felt he was a disgrace in family eyes as his family and they were aware of the way he lived. Suddenly there was a knock at the door and as he opened the door he could see it was his sister who was stood before him and his eldest niece was with her mother. His sister Mary hugged him, and his niece Caitlin gave him a kiss on his cheek. George held back the tears, they drove to Mary's village in the Hampshire countryside George felt it was just what he needed because in London he would have only locked himself away apart from his binge drinking. At the same time George was on his break, scattered all over the country teams of terrorists were by now travelling to their nominated targets. One team only had to travel a short very distance to their nominated target some of the others had many miles to travel to get to their designated destinations. One or two travelled the previous day they all knew the date and the time they were to carry out their objectives. That evening George enjoyed a very restful night's sleep because the room he slept in was just like a hotel room. When he awoke the following morning, he took a long hot shower the sun was pouring into the room, he thought to himself life could not be any better. After he showered he dressed and went downstairs to where his sister's family were sat around a large kitchen table eating breakfast. Mary's husband Dave enquired if George slept well and he replied, "I certainly did it was great, and I must say you are spoiling me thank you". His niece Caitlin spoke "mum said she wanted to spoil you". George smiled at her and replied, "well she has certainly done that" he once again thanked everyone. Dave said his goodbyes and he left to get off to work. With that Mary took George and Caitlin into town. At the same time and in the same town a train from London just pulled into the station and two men stepped off the train both were carrying large travel bags. The men looked like any other normal person in other words and did not stand out from the crowd. They walked out of the railway station and didn't raise any suspicions as they both looked like any other young men, but these two had evil intent in their hearts. They walked down the hill and into town it was by now late morning the sun was out in all its glory filling the blue sky. The historic town looked resplendent bathed in the bright sun. The two men walked into town and found themselves a café to grab a bite to eat and a drink. The waitress brought their order to their table. One of the men asked her for the directions to the bus station, she was extremely polite and gave them directions and the men thanked her. Little did she know she was looking directly into the eyes of two killers. They duly paid their bill and had left a tip. They walked towards the bus station and they checked the bus time table to check what time the bus departed for their intended target. They noted the time and could see they still had an hour or so to while away the time as they did not want to arrive at their target too early because they would stand out a mile in a village setting. In town they could easily blend in as tourists. But inside their maddening minds they had only wanted to use public transport because if their mission went wrong in any way they could still kill and maim anyone innocently travelling on the same bus as the pair of them. Elsewhere all the other cells were travelling towards their designated targets. They were also carrying the murderous tools to enable them to carry out their hideous acts of violence. All ten cells were issued with the same equipment and were all trained to use it. The cells were travelling to very similar sites. It was a Friday and lots of people had begun to relax and they were looking forward to a relaxing weekend after working very hard during the week. People were starting to gather at pubs and restaurants across the country. It was soon time for the cells to survey their nominated targets. The two men checked their watches and boarded the bus which would convey them to their nominated village and their target. Night time was beginning to fall, and it was getting darker, all the better to act under the cover of darkness. The "controller" chose the targets because of one significant reason and it was because the British Government had cut the strength of the British police force and he guessed correctly that the villages he chose as targets would not have police patrolling partly due to the severe cut backs. Both terrorists soon alighted from the bus they thanked the driver for dropping them off in the village where they would soon carry act their hideous acts of violence. They headed for the village recreation ground and the summer night sky began to descend the recreation ground was by now in darkness luckily no one was around besides they were wearing dark clothing and blended in the darkness. The pair previously studied various maps of the village online and they knew roughly where there was a small wood, between the recreation ground and the village pub. They soon found the wood and entered it and while they were within the cover of the wood they each took from their bags a suicide vest, the vests were filled with explosives, nails, nuts and bolts including a detonator which was attached to the vests, an AK47, Kalashnikov rifle with extra magazines loaded with extra rounds of ammunition. They exited the wood and soon headed across the pub carpark one of the men approached the rear of the pub and headed towards a rear door leading into the pubs restaurant area. To the left he could see some log cabin rooms the terrorists weren't interested in the rooms it was the packed bar area and the restaurant they were most interested in. Their mission was solely to attack the pub and to kill as many people as possible. As one of the men approached the rear door the other man approached the front door. He could see through the pub windows he observed the pub was packed to the rafters. He quickly checked his watch there was just under a minute to go, the other terrorists, would be approaching their nominated targets by now. As one of the terrorists was approaching the front door and he noticed a concrete patio in front of the pub and he quickly checked, no one was sat drinking outside on the patio. At the same time sitting inside Mary's sitting room George was talking to Mary, he was due to go to the village pub with her husband Dave as soon as he arrived home from work. Just then the phone rang, and it was Dave he informed Mary his train had been delayed by about an hour and he told her to let George know for him to go to the pub ahead of him and he would catch up with him a bit later. George said, "its ok Mary I will stay here and keep you company" she told him not to worry and to go and enjoy himself up at the pub. George walked up the hill leading to the pub. As he approached the patio area of the pub he could hear rifle shots being an ex soldier, one never forgets the sound of a rifle having been discharged in a confined space. Suddenly, he heard screams coming from inside the pub he could hear more screams and people inside pleading for help and mercy. He noticed an iron bar laying on the ground on the patio just outside of the pub and he quickly picked it up then he gently began to open the door to the pub and he immediately saw some bodies slumped on the tiled floor and in front of the bar blood was splattered all over the place and bits of brain matter was covering a mirror behind the bar. He quickly assessed the situation he saw in front of him. He slowly moved further into the bar area and he could see a gunman with his back towards him so he gripped the iron bar tightly in his hand and he raised the bar in the air and brought the metal bar crashing down with all his might onto the man's head and he felt the bar cave the gunman's head in and as it smashed into his skull he could feel the bar cracking open the man's skull as it sank into the soft material within his skull, the man screamed out luckily the sounds coming from the gunman was drowned out by the screams emanating from amongst the dead and the dying who were sprawled out on the floor, many with horrendous looking gunshot wounds. When he turned the gunman onto his back he needed to grab hold of the terrorist's rifle slung across his chest George soon realised the gunman was wearing a suicide vest and let's just say he soon made sure the man was dead, he grabbed hold of the rifle and very quietly walked towards the other gunman who was by now in the restaurant, still firing his rifle at the diners.

George did not need to get too close to him and he took aim at the man holding a rifle and shot the gunman in the face he just could not risk the gunman setting off his suicide vest. If he had just wounded the gunman man, he might have been able to detonate the vest he was wearing. People within the restaurant were screaming and some were clearly in a state of shock George picked up the other man's rifle and when he took a look at the man's face part of it was obliterated and he then took the rifle from the body he then dragged the man's body towards the rear door and dumped it outside he then rushed to the front of the bar and dragged the first terrorist out of the front door and onto the patio there was blood everywhere there was also a trail of blood where George dragged the bodies along the tiled floor and out of the pub door. He phoned 999 when he got through to someone they told him someone else in the pub already phoned regarding the attack. He went to help and assist the many casualties and very soon the pub was surrounded by armed police and as they entered the pub George handed over the two rifles he briefed them on what he saw and what he did whereupon he was arrested for the killing of the two terrorists. Some of the survivors pleaded with the police having pointed out to them it wasn't George who attacked the pub, some people shouted at the police if hadn't been for George they would all be dead now. A policeman told the survivors because George used excessive force and he should have only used minimum force, he should have wounded the two men. George said as he was being arrested and placed in hand cuffs "you are all fucking idiots can't you see the two men are wearing suicide vests and would have set them off". He was soon placed into a police car and driven off for further questioning only to be locked up in the police cells. The paramedics were soon on the scene. The pub looked like a scene from a horror film. At the same time in nine other sleepy country villages across the country the same scene was unfolding and some of the terrorists managed to set off their suicide vests with such disastrous consequences. In two of the other villages the terrorists also attacked the village pubs and then casually walked around the villages shooting anyone who came out of their houses to investigate what the commotion was about for some it was the very last thing they ever did in this world. Some were dead, and some people also had their throats slit. It was carnage and when the terrorists ran out of ammunition they blew themselves up causing even more carnage. That same evening the news coverage was about the attacks across the country the headlines were the same "The UK is under sustained attack by Terrorists". The home secretary appeared on the TV he asked for the public to remain calm as the police had the situation under control? Not many people believed anything the government were telling them, they were being lied to by the government for many years. The public endured food poverty for a couple of years and now the latest attacks were the last straw. That same evening the Prime Minister was presiding over an emergency COBR, Cabinet Briefing Rooms, held in the cabinet office in Whitehall. The COBR meeting is designed to make fast and effective decisions during a major crisis. Reports were soon arriving first reports indicated there was approximately 83 deaths and over one hundred people injured. The police confirmed at least twenty terrorists had also been killed mostly suicides, but there was a report coming in of two terrorists having been killed by a former soldier a military veteran. The prime minister suddenly turned very pale the blood seemed to have drained from his face when he heard of the figures he knew straight away his government would fall and very soon because of the terrorist attacks on innocent people. The Metropolitan Police Commissioner briefed the meeting about what she knew regarding the terrorist attacks, many of the attacks were targeted on village pubs including two community centres one of which was holding a wedding reception. The terrorists deliberately targeted areas of the countryside where there was little, or no police presence she went on to explain the terrorists had seemingly done their homework extremely well. The Prime Minister knew his own ideologic political policies helped to allow the atrocities to happen. All his nightmares were happening seemingly all at once. The head of MI5 briefed the PM regarding a person who was detained during one of the attacks and that person was George. The MI5 obtained some CCTV images of the terrorists using public transport and apart from George each terrorist had been accounted for because they were killed at the scene of their horrific crimes. In the case of George, he was immediately released from custody. A barrister who had been saved by George's selfless act of courage in the pub travelled to the police station and he helped to explain to the desk sergeant George was in fact a hero and not a terrorist and if he hadn't killed the terrorists in the manner he had, the terrorists would have had the time to set off their suicide vests they were wearing. The detective in charge spoke to the QC and after he vouched for George he was immediately released from custody and his release had been authorised at the very top of the Police force. When George was eventually dropped off at his sister's house by the police Mary hugged him and Caitlin said, "oh uncle George you are a hero" George looked at her and said, "what do you means sweetheart?" Dave explained "George we know all about what you did at the pub, it's all over the news also a barrister from the village has been on the news explaining about what happened and how the police arrested you he went on to explain about how you saved so many lives tonight" George did not know what to say he was aghast he was very modest man. Mary hugged him "oh George you are very brave man" and with that they sat around the kitchen table and had a stiff drink and for a moment they all sat in silence, to reflect, and to think about those who were not so lucky.

Back in Whitehall some politicians within the government had realised because of the prime minister ideological and personal views, the country was suffering badly. But not one of his ministers opposed him and if they had he would have sacked the minister showing any decent towards his leadership. The terrorist outrages were the last straw and things in government would have to change and soon. In America as soon as the President got to hear about the atrocities in the United Kingdom he immediately spoke to the vice president his first words were "that fucking man thinks of others, such as terrorists, rather than his own people he has to be goddam removed and soon". The vice president totally agreed with him. The cards were heavily stacked against the British Prime minister and it was his own making he could not blame anyone else but himself, he might have wanted to offload the blame but not now. The British opposition parties slowly got their act together and were a viable opposition to the government's policies. Meanwhile the coward "controller" who based in the middle east had suddenly dropped off the radar, disappeared into thin air. The middle east at the time was an area of spies and counter spies and riddled with espionage and most of the western nations security services used spies and double agents. Israel was sometimes left to clean up the mess on their doorstep, left by western security services. There was no doubt that the so called "goodies" had known of the "controller" and it was possibly they may have used his services in one mode or another. Not forgetting the British government who had possibly inadvertently funded the "controller" or an affiliated organisation with British tax payer's money from the foreign aid budget how ironic. Post the terrorist attacks the British government were under extreme pressure to stand down from government. The Home secretary was the sacrificial lamb and he immediately resigned from his position in government, but it hadn't been enough. The Russian president was shocked at the news to the very recent attacks in Britain even though he once planned to inflict yet another war upon the people's, of Europe? But it is modern politics changing tact form one day to another.   At the headquarters of the Metropolitan Police Headquarters in London the IT department flagged up a civil servant who was currently working within the department and managed to copy a document onto a memory stick and sent the document to the cloud network. It was a very serious breach of security and it hadn't taken very long to highlight the breach only because both the user and the computer had a high level of security and users could down load documents onto an official and approved memory stick only if they had been security cleared the breach was found during a routine weekly security check on the Mets IT equipment. The IT manager duly informed a police inspector regarding the breach of security the IT department had managed to identify the email and the attachment they and then identified the user id and more specifically to the actual computer. The letter which had been copied was the Home secretaries recent letter to the Metropolitan Police Commissioner the document was classified of a very sensitive nature. The Police Inspector asked the IT manager to meet with her in her office with all the evidence he had managed to gather. After the meeting she requested an urgent meeting with the Commissioner. She took the IT departments evidence to the commissioner. The Commissioner soon realised there was a "spy" working within the Headquarters she also knew the identity of the so called "spy. It was time to "lift" him to find out who he was supplying confidential information to. When he was being interviewed and under caution he soon broke down in tears he told the investigators he didn't think it what he did would ever harm anyone as he was only doing what he believed in. It wasn't until he was told what he did made him complicit in at least 83 deaths and countless injured. He sobbed his heart out and at his trail he was sentenced to life in prison. The "controller" wasn't interested in the "spies" he had recruited as they were only pawns in a much bigger picture. Awamiri was staying with family in London and keeping a very low profile. He saw on the news the details of the recent terrorist atrocities the police had also publicly let it be known that a "mole" in the Metropolitan police was recently sentenced to life in prison. As he sat watching the news he thought to himself "well if the police had any link between the terrorists and myself they would have surely arrested me by now". But unknown to him the net was slowly closing in on him, slowly but surely. In the middle east the "controller" was picked up by the Israeli Mossad security agents, he was on their radar for a couple years the Mossad agents were living in various countries in the middle east and their colleagues in the MI6 including the CIA wanted the "controller" lifted for questioning. Mossad decided to pick him up at his flat, he was living in a volatile area of the middle east and if he had been "lifted" on the streets things would get violent. He was subdued with a drug and was soon being bundled into a waiting car at the rear of the house and driven to an old airfield and eventually flown out of the area by military helicopter to Israel. The agents who lived in the area for many years felt secure enough to search his flat for terrorist related evidence that would link him to the killings in the UK and of course to many other terrorist incidents across the world. They soon discovered mobile phones and a couple of laptops. Because they also found various of interest items it was decided to rip the apartment apart. In the bathroom as one of the agents walked over a floor tile she noticed some of the tiles were cemented down recently and were uneven they were roughly the size of a laptop. She prised some of the tiles up and discovered a laptop wrapped in bubble wrap. She called out to the other two agents "bingo got it". They continued with the search and found some notebooks contained inside were what the agents thought were mobile phone numbers All the items were placed into the agents backpacks they couldn't just walk out of the building with the items on display they were operating in a hostile area with many militia who would not think twice about slitting the throats of a mossad agent.   They moved along the road outside the apartment and jumped into their 4x4 jeep and quickly drove away from the area. There was an another mossad agent who operated out of a shop in the same area on roof of the shop was a radio and he spoke to the mossad headquarters in Tel Aviv Israel and asked for another military helicopter to fly to his area of operations his agents recovered some interesting items, in the "controllers" flat. The helicopter arrived at the very same disused airfield this time under the cover of darkness the items which were discovered were soon loaded into the helicopter and flown out of the country and into the safety of Israel for further analysis.

The "controller" was housed in a cell below a none descript building in the centre of Tel Aviv. The mossad computer geeks quickly broke into the laptop and it took a further day or two to break into a password account and the subsequent security gates. As soon as the, IT bods broke into the Laptop they thought "my god this is all our Christmases in one hit". One of the geeks called out to the other agents "bingo" and he was able to track the "controller" on the dark web and the trace led them to Awamiri based in Birmingham in the UK. Contained on the laptop were the many details of the terrorist groups who recently bombed the UK and how they had managed to slip into the UK the contacts of those who allowed their homes to be used as safe houses for the terrorist he had recorded the addresses and contact telephone numbers including the home holder's names. The laptop contained details of other terrorist cells in Europe mainly in Germany, Belgium and France. The Israeli security services found an interesting email from an IP address with in the Metropolitan Police in London. The email included contained an attachment from the British Home Secretary. In Britain many in the country were up in arms regarding the recent terrorist atrocities the government was feeling a backlash regarding the terrorist events. It was the last straw. Major questions were being asked of the government more so of the prime minister and the cabinet. The opposition were by now beginning to make the government feel extremely uncomfortable and were finally bringing the government to account and soon demanded a general election to topple the government. There were calls for the country's borders to be immediately closed and to all free moving migration. The Home Secretary did not have a choice but to close the country's open borders, it was obvious the terrorist had bypassed the open border points and so easily smuggled themselves into the UK, undetected. More resources were found to patrol the open coastal area across the English Channel, it was all too little and far too late. All ten terrorist who carried out the attacks on innocent people that Friday night had either blown themselves up or shot themselves when they had run out of ammunition apart from the two terrorists George killed during the terrorist attack in his sister's village. Meanwhile MI6 were sent the various files found on the "controllers" laptop the files had been sent by Mossad based in Israel. The director of MI5 was given hard copies of the files which were found, and he and his deputy were sat in his office reading through the various documents found and they made for very interesting reading. Richard the director's deputy was sat reading through some of the Arabic documents and spoke up "fuck sake some of this information could bring down the bloody Prime Minister" Mark replied, "yes I know this is a bloody fine mess, a viper's nest, leading to heart of the British government". Mark picked up the phone on his desk he spoke directly with the prime minister "Prime Minister we need to meet and urgently I have some information which has been found on a terrorist, lifted in the middle east". He spent the next couple of minutes saying "yes" and once the call was over he put the phone down. He looked at Richard and said, "make sure we save the files somewhere much more secure, I think we need to protect our backs on this one". Mark was sure Mossad would have sent copies of the same files to their American counter parts. Contained within one of the files there was a document from a Whitehall department from the Foreign and Aid department the document confirmed with an organisation based in the middle east and it was an organisation backed by the Prime Minister the government had recently allocated £2.5 million pounds to the said organisation. It was an organisation who were known to be paying terrorist groups and it was the same group the "controller" belonged to before his arrest in the middle east. In Israel the same group, British aid was funding and it was a banned terrorist group and a well-known terrorist organisation in the middle east and it was known for training suicide bombers. Mark and Richard walked over to the prime minister's office in No 10 Downing Street with the documents in a secure briefcase. They were let into the building and were escorted to the prime minister's office. Inside the prime minister was sat with the minister of defence and the minister for security. Mark began the briefing by outlining the known information they knew about the terrorist known as the "controller" who was caught and arrested by Mossad in the middle east. He showed the Julien the various documents

Richard also had the documents translated from Arabic into English. The prime minister read the documents and once he finished reading them he then handed them to the other ministers, sat in the room, to read. Julien spoke to the two men who were sat in front of him and asked Mark "apart from the Israelis who else knows about this and do you think we can keep it from the press"? Mark said to him "well the CIA will have by now read the documents it's the way Mossad work and no doubt the American President will have been fully briefed by now, and we do not have any influence with Mossad or the CIA, more so with the food embargo and the Naval blockade by NATO, Intelligence wise we are completely blind". The pair left Downing street still with the documents and as they walked to the MI6 building Mark said to Richard "I think this could bring down the government".

In his office the prime minister spoke to his ministers "gentlemen I do not think the British people will ever forgive any of us sat in this office for tax payer's money having helped to fund terrorists and our own people being murdered by the same people who were being paid to do so with the same British tax payers money, we must be prepared for the consequences of our own actions". Meanwhile the British police were joined by members of MI5 and MI6 they raided each one of the safe houses identified on the "controllers" laptop. Found inside some of the houses was substantial amounts of material implicating the house holders in facilitating the act of terrorism it proved beyond any doubt that they had been heavily involved with providing safe houses to the terrorists. Inside some of the houses the police found bundles of cash it was all found hidden under the floor boards, no doubt part of the money paid to organisations in the middle east and funded by the British government from the overseas aid budget. A resident of one of the houses being searched was upstairs in one of the bedrooms he would not come downstairs and one of the MI5 agents together with an armed policeman tried to get upstairs, but a woman suddenly appeared at the top of the stairs and she began to shout at the officers in Arabic. The MI5 officer understood some Arabic he soon realised she was in fact shouting out a warning to someone inside one of the bedrooms. The agent and the police officer barged their way past the woman and entered a bedroom only to find a man speaking into a mobile and he was also speaking in Arabic the agent only caught the end of the call "quick I must go they are here". The agent grabbed the man and took the mobile from the man, the policeman aimed his rifle at the man who complied with the two men and he was placed in hand cuffs by the police man. They took him downstairs and by this time the woman was in hysterics she started to slap the policeman around the face. A female detective placed the woman in cuffs and she led the woman out of the house and as she did so the woman shouted at the detective in English "you won't hear the last of this, all of you will be eradicated from this land" and with that she was placed into an unmarked police car the man arrested inside the house was placed into another unmarked police car the pair were driven to an unknown destination within London. The MI5 officer made a call to his control room he reported what he had found and recounted the incident of the man in the bedroom he told them that he thought the man may have tipped off perhaps the person who may have organised the logistics for the ten terrorists who went on to carry out the recent attacks. The organiser might now be on the way to a port or airport. It would not take too long for MI5 and the police to be on heightened alert watching all ports and airports, but one thing they didn't have it was a description of the person they were looking for. They needed a break through, regarding the "organiser" and they desperately needed a description of who they were looking for. Indeed, Awamiri had in fact been tipped off by the man in the safe house before he was arrested. He was feeling confident and upbeat, he was safe only because he hadn't been arrested. Once again, he needed to destroy the pay as you go mobile phone, and as he walked past a building site he could see a bonfire close to a footpath and it was where workmen were burning odd cuts of wood and some wooden pallets he observed no one was around the site and he quickly threw the mobile phone including its SIM card which was still inside the phone into the embers of the fire, it was his first mistake. On the SIM card was the list of the recent phone calls including the one from the man who was recently arrested at a safe house the phone had an incoming call from the "controller" before he was "lifted" by the mossad agents in the middle east. Once Awamiri had left the area of the bonfire, a labourer from the building site saw a man throwing something into the bonfire and he left the shelter of a portacabin he picked up a stick and as he approached the fire he could just make out a mobile phone and he managed to drag the by now melted mobile out from the hot embers of the fire and he left it in the mud to eventually cool down. An hour later he came back, and he took the mobile into the works portacabin and he left it in his locker and thought nothing more of it. That was until a Metropolitan police spokesman gave a press conference regarding the recent terrorist attacks. During the press conference he informed the public many ordinary people within the midlands were helping the police with their enquiries. He went on to explain the police required even more help from the public regarding the young men who carried out the recent despicable terrorist attacks and it seemed the terrorists travelled on public transport and they all carried very similar bags and holdalls a picture of the type of bag flashed up on the TV screen, the police officer went on to explain the men and a couple of women were travelling in pairs and were possibly speaking in Arabic. He showed the type of pay as you go mobile phones the police had thought was used to communicate with one another. He asked if people could look inside their bins and garden bonfires to see if any of the mobiles had been destroyed by fire or may have been thrown into random rubbish bins. The young labourer Simon hadn't been paying too much notice to the news on the TV until the mention of mobile phones and bonfires he took a quick look at the type of mobile phone the police were interested in; the picture of the phone was displayed on the screen. Simon told his dad "I found one of those types of phones in a bonfire at the building site today". His dad looked at his son and said, "what the bloody hell are you waiting for son phone the police now". Simon began to shake, he contacted the police's non-emergency telephone number he explained about finding the mobile. They took his details and the lady informed him someone would be in contact with him in a day or two. But less than an hour after Simon contacted the police there was a knock at the front door of his parents' home. His mother went to answer the knock and when she opened the door she was confronted by two smartly dressed men who brandished their identity cards they introduced themselves as MI5 agents following up on her son's recent phone call to the police. She invited them into the house and took them to the rear of the house into the kitchen where Simon and his dad were sat at the kitchen table. His mum Anne introduced the agents to her husband John and of course Simon. His father said, "bloody hell what's he done". The two men introduced themselves and once again they produced their ID cards. One of the men said, "your son hasn't done anything wrong we are following up his call to the police". His dad turned towards his son "well done son" the agents asked Simon if he could take them to where he worked so they could look at the area and the bonfire. John said, "go on son you might be the link to those bastards who killed all those poor people". Simons mum said, "oh Simon well done for making the call to the police". He and the two agents soon jumped into a waiting car and they sped off to where he worked when they arrived at the building site he had a key to the portacabin and when they were inside he took them to his area of the portacabin and sat inside his locker was the mobile phone it looked a little worse for wear. One of the agents placed the mobile inside an evidence bag for further forensic checks. The other agent said, "I don't suppose he wasn't so stupid as to have left the SIM card in the phone has his"? Simon piped up "I don't know it might still be inside the mobile because the bonfire was well alight when I saw the man throwing it into the fire. The officer holding the bag said, "what you actually saw the man throwing the bloody mobile into the fire" and he replied, "oh yes and not only that I filmed him doing it on my mobile". One of the agents asked him if he would accompany them to MI5 headquarters. Simon could not contain his excitement "great no problems I just need to phone my parents and my boss". One of the agents replied, "please phone your parents but we shall contact your boss so don't worry about him". Simon duly phoned his parents. When all three arrived at MI5 headquarters the agents handed the burnt mobile to another agent who was the duty technician. Simon was taken to an interview room to provide a statement regarding the time leading up to the man throwing the mobile into the fire to and what Simon did with the mobile after he had retrieved it from the fire.

The agent taking the statement suddenly had to leave the room and in a corridor his boss was fast approaching him, the agent briefed him on the initial findings regarding the burnt mobile "we have found the SIM card it was still intact, the technicians are downloading data found on it. However, the young man's mobile has film of the man who had been seen throwing the mobile into the fire. The film is good, but the suspects face isn't very sharp, it is still useable. You will need to ask the young man if we have permission to wipe his phone clean of all its data and film, we cannot have the film evidence falling into the hands of the press". The agent spoke once again to Simon about the film on his mobile and he eventually gave permission for it to be wiped clean. The agents dropped Simon and his mobile back home. The MI5 officers contacted both Simon's boss at his work place and the management at the building company. The CEO of the company decided to personally phone Simon at home and he told Simon he was very proud of him, obviously his boss hadn't been told everything about the case but a senior officer at MI5 explained as much as he needed to know and no more. In his youth Simon was a bit of a lad. For his parents they were very proud of what he had done and to now have the CEO of his company phoned him at home was the icing on the cake. At MI5 headquarters the technicians were working very hard on trying to enhance the film taken of what could have been Awamiri throwing a mobile into the bonfire. As soon as the technicians enhanced the film the only thing they were unable to make any clearer was the man's face. His clothing and his build were enhanced and made sharper. One of the technicians could just make out a small ring on the suspects small finger. He managed to enlarge the finger including the ring. It was a ring with some Arabic writing, but it was too blurred to read. It was by now two am in the morning the deputy of MI5 called for an urgent meeting with the head of the laboratory and the two agents who were leading on the case. The head of the laboratory managed to print the data found on the burnt mobile's SIM card. Some of the data on the SIM card was in Arabic and it was soon translated into English. The man arrested in the midlands was found to have phoned the burnt mobile yet again there was a connection to the "controller" the mobile used by Awamiri had indeed made a call to the mobile found by mossad in the middle east. The police and the security forces had to quickly find the man still on the run in the UK and quickly. By now Awamiri travelled by train to the South West of England. The Police released a statement regarding the continuing manhunt for a key suspect linked to the recent terrorist attacks. They released the film footage of the man throwing a mobile phone into the fire at the building site they also released a still photograph of the ring the man was wearing. The press release was released to each daily newspaper. It was a matter of utmost urgency he was found and quickly. In Winchester the young waitress who served the two terrorists before attacking the pub in a local village. She remembered the two men because she was so sure while in the cafe they spoke in a foreign language possibly Arabic she could not be so sure but one thing she did know it wasn't, English. She decided to contact the police and they visited her at her place of work they enquired if the café had any CCTV overage the café manager confirmed they had CCTV coverage. The police took the DVD recordings with them and asked if the young woman could come with them to their police station because if the terrorists had been recorded they needed her to identify the two men. It took a few hours to trawl through the many hours of film footage, the café did not have an index system and so the police had to trawl through many of the DVD's. As they viewed a section of CCTV the woman told the person who was looking at the film with her to stop and said, "that's them the two men". The police thanked her for assisting them in their investigation and got her to write a statement once she was ready to leave the police station they handed her the other DVD's. They kept the DVD showing the two men to use as evidence. The police copied the frames with the men featured and sent the files via email to the metropolitan police. The Winchester police typed up a statement with the information the waitress supplied especially when the two men asked for directions to the bus station. The number sixteen bus would have been the bus that would take the pair to the village where they were about to attack. The police soon managed to trace the bus driver who drove the bus to the village he confirmed he had remembered the two men and he thought he may have dropped the pair off very close to the village recreation ground. The police sent a report to the Metropolitan police. The Met were desperately trying to build a picture of all ten teams movements on the day of the attacks. The Met operations teams were also feeding information to both MI5 and MI6.

Chapter 8 – Caught

So far there hadn't been any further information regarding the "Organiser", Awamiri. But unknown to the police he was hiding in Devon because he had been waiting to catch the ferry from Plymouth over to Spain. As he was checking the sailing timetable, at the ferry port, to see when the next ferry crossing to Spain was leaving port he saw the sailings were only weekly and he had three days to wait for the next ferry crossing, he had to find a cheap B&B, bed and breakfast. He had two nights to keep a low profile and when he paid the landlady cash she could not help but notice the small gold signet ring he was wearing with some sort of writing on it she noticed he was wearing it on one of his small fingers. She remembered the police appeal on the national news. She knew the police were desperately trying to locate the last known terrorist who they thought was on the run in the UK. She saw the police film showing a man throwing something into a bonfire she also saw the still pictures of the man's small finger wearing a signet ring. She acted calmly and showed him to his room and let him know the timings for breakfast, he thanked her and asked where the nearest fish and chip shop was. She gave him the directions to the closest one and with that she went back downstairs. He soon left the B&B and as she watched him walking in the direction of the fish and chip shop she felt safe enough to contact the police when she made the call she told them about what had just happened. She was told not to panic and to try and to carry on as normal going about her normal business and not to panic and to try and not spook the suspect. Ten minutes later she was contacted by phone it was the police she was informed an undercover armed unit would book in at the

Caught

B&B as guests, they would need a room the team would consist of a man and a woman and they will be dressed in plain clothes. Twenty minutes later the pair soon turned up and they were stood at reception booking a room, just as Awamiri entered the building and he spoke to the landlady he said to the her "the fish and chips were very nice" just as the couple turned to face him and it was at this point he realised his time was up the female officer pulled out her police issued pistol at the same time the policeman forced Awamiri to the ground and he quickly hand cuffed him and once they secured him he was then searched for a weapon and any possible explosives luckily for everyone he was unarmed. The police woman radioed informing other police officers waiting outside that the suspect was arrested and handcuffed and subdued. Other uniformed police officers poured into the B&B and searched his room they brought his bag and his passport downstairs and loaded him into an unmarked police car the two undercover officers took their prisoner with his belongings to the local police station. At the police station he was finger printed his eyes were photographed with a biometric machine and scanned through the National Police computer it was found he had never been involved with the police and as such hadn't been recorded on the police database, that was up until now. The police informed MI5 and MI6 of his arrest. The police were told to hold him overnight in a cell until the following morning when a team of agents would be in Plymouth and they would arrange to transport for him to travel back to London. In the police cell Awamiri hadn't said a word to the police he knew full well his time was well and truly up. During the night the police kept him on suicide watch his clothes were taken off him and bagged as evidence and all his orifices were searched and it was not a pleasant job, but it was a very important one. The police were looking for a suicide capsule or something else which could assist him in carrying out a suicide attempt. Later he was dressed in a police force issued all in one suit a blue attire. The following morning two armed MI5 officers turned up at the police station to take the prisoner to London for further questioning. During the same period some of those killed during the recent terrorist atrocities. Their bodies WERE released by the coroner's office to their families for burial. The various funerals across the country were covered on the national news channels it was an emotional time for all those concerned. In Winchester George was invited by some of the relatives whose family members who were tragically killed in the village pub he had visited on that fateful night and he gratefully accepted the funeral invite, it was the least he could do. George attended one of the funerals he was given a standing ovation by all those attending and of course George was so embarrassed, he could not take it all in and all because one minute he was an old ex military veteran sitting in his local pub in London to being praised as a hero, it was all too much for him to take in. It was no good going back to London as he was still helping the police with their enquiries in Hampshire. The Prime Minister Julien Jones and his government's ministers were hanging onto power only by the skin of their teeth. He managed in just three and half years to bring the country to its knees and almost bankrupted it. The opposition were as much to blame and were just as culpable for not bringing the government to account and to help bring the government crashing down. All the British politicians at the time hadn't served the country or the people with any distinction. Awamiri eventually attended Westminster Crown Court on various terrorism charges he was eventually sentenced to life in prison. He told all attending the court he did not recognise the court or the British Crown or the state of Britain. Attending the day of sentencing were so many of the victims from the villages where the terrorists caused so much sadness on that fateful Friday. On hearing the Judges summing up and the life sentence handed down to Awamiri, the relatives and the friends of many of the victims, clapped but there wasn't any shouting or jeering from the public gallery only the sounds of gentle and muffled clapping. The "controller" was still being held in Israel may not be so lucky as to get away with a life sentence. Because many years previously the state of Israel gave a preliminary approval for courts to impose the death sentence for terrorism and later in 2019 it was passed as law. The Israelis had enough evidence for the "controller" to be linked to many terrorist attacks on Israel. Mossad reported to the Prime Minister of Israel and pointed out it was Britain and its Foreign Overseas Aid budget which was funding the man nicknamed the "controller" who directed the terrorist cells in Britain. The Prime Minister in turn lodged a serious diplomatic complaint to the British Prime Minister pointing out Britain was funding various international terrorist organisations within the middle east. The "controller" was at last put on trial in an Israeli military court on various terrorism charges, eventually he was found guilty and hung for his crimes. His sentence was never made public and during his time in custody he never once gave any details not even his real name, or his date of birth or his place of birth. His laptop provided security forces across the world with so much information and it was invaluable. It enabled the French police to close the arms smuggling route into the UK. Belgium police forces were able to close the many safe houses in and around the capital Brussels. Russia was contacted regarding the supply of Arms, ammunition and military explosive material having been sold on the black market by various Russian Army Regiments. It was the same with the Ukrainian security services. It was soon time for George to return to his dingy bedsit in London his sister Mary drove him to London. When he opened the door to his room the landlord was in the building he shook Georges hand and said "welcome back mate, in my eyes you are a bloody hero" he handed him a stack of mail it was all addressed to George the landlord promptly left the room. Mary looked over at him they both smiled. He made Mary a cup of tea and as they sat drinking their cup of tea he threw the junk mail onto the floor as he sorted the junk mail from the bills. He was left with a couple of bills amongst the bills was an official looking envelope with a couple of official looking rubber stamps on the front of the envelope. Just before he ripped the envelope open Mary spoke "George stop look the envelope has a Downing Street rubber stamp on it". He looked puzzled and instead of just ripping at the envelope he began to open it very carefully and he pulled out a letter and began to read the very formal looking letter, as he did so his face drained of colour he began to shake uncontrollably. His sister gently took the letter from his hand and she read its contents. She suddenly said, "oh bloody hell George you have only been awarded the George Cross medal for your unselfish bravery against two heavily armed and lethal terrorists without unselfishly giving any thought about your own safety". All he could say in reply was "I know how bloody mad that is". He turned to Mary and said, "I need a bloody strong drink". She replied George "let's go to your local" she knew he was a heavy drinker but when he was staying at her house he had laid off the booze and apart from the night at her village pub even then, he didn't get a chance to have a drink. As they walked into the pub the landlord said "bloody hell the returning hero well done George the drinks are on me" George introduced his sister to him and as they were drinking their drinks the landlady appeared at the bar and she said the same as the landlord. Mary spoke "George go on tell them your good news" he pushed out his chest and replied, "I have been awarded The George Cross in the latest honours list" they both said in unison "bloody hell good on you, you deserve it well done mate". He asked for a whisky and he drank it straight back in one gulp Mary also had a soft drink and after the drinks they both left the pub. Later in the day Mary drove home and George stayed at his bedsit he decided he needed to clean his room and had an early night it was a little too much to take in. It wasn't too long before the British opposition parties in parliament had at last banded together to form a coalition with more MPs, Member of Parliament, than the government. It meant the opposition could at last vote most bills down the governments legislation put before the house. It wasn't too long before there was a vote of no confidence in the sitting British Government. The government's own party had been infighting there were many internal splits within Julien's party and it didn't look good for the government. The writing was on the wall and they knew it. Within the houses of parliament, a no confidence motion was put before ministers it read very much along the similar lines as the last motion of no confidence in the government in 1979 "this house has no confidence in Her Majesty's Government". It was a rare motion to put before the government as mentioned the previous motion was in 1979 and before then it was back in 1924. It now meant there would have to be a general election. In Moscow the Russian President Anatoly Petrov thanked his lucky stars he hadn't "purchased" the UK ports and military air bases. Things in the UK were precarious to say the least. Potentially things could not be any worse in the country. The recent terrorist attacks had only gone to help prove the country there was no control of anyone entering and living in the country. Now the government and the Prime Minister had been voted down and had been a huge vote of no confidence. The Russian president knew he had narrowly missed an opportunity to wage war on Europe. He also realised the Americans would be avidly watching what was going on during the upcoming British general election. Meanwhile China kept well away from influencing future British politics and the Chinese premier was so relieved his country backed out of using British ports and military air bases. Most of the British public were by now so fed up with rationing and lack of food there had been so many rumours and by this time the country was on the verge of bankruptcy. It was all too much for people to take because there had to be a change in British politics and very soon. Julien Jones the Prime Minister brought the country to its knees all because of his own idiotic ideology for people living in the 21st century his political and revolutionary ideas came from a bygone era from the 1970's and he came to realise and came to his senses but it was far too late, his seemingly fondness of terrorist organisations including the gross misuse of the Foreign Overseas Aid budget was against the wishes of the vast majority of people in the UK. The country's gold reserve was all but spent and the country was tottering on the brink of bankruptcy. Life for the ordinary citizen was becoming extremely unbearable. It was almost as if someone had got hold of a giant paint brush and painted the country in grey paint. In Moscow Sergei was sat at his desk in the FSB headquarters. When he noticed a message arriving his message in box on his computer it was from the head of the FSB's Cyber director and he ordered Sergei to pull his agent Alexei from the case in Belgium and to block the veteran's social media access to every Russian citizens because the President had now deemed it a subversive site and as such it was now banned in Russia. Sergei read the message and he thought to himself "oops someone or something has upset the President". He duly carried out the orders and two days later he heard from a friend within the FSB every one of the Russian Veterans who were members of the social media group were recently rounded

Caught

up and were held in various prisons for crimes against the state. They were eventually tried in a military court and within days were handed various lengthy sentences all to be served in military prisons. Ivor was sentenced to ten years hard labour for his so called "crimes against the state" he knew he would never leave prison alive. Suddenly, the Frenchman François appeared on the social media site and once again spouted his mouth off about the French government and their policies. He hadn't been active on the site for over a year. He made a comment regarding Ivor he observed that all the other Russian veterans had suddenly dropped off the radar. He seemed to be taking a more of an interest in the Russian veterans. In America Sam heard about George having been awarded the George Cross for bravery. Word soon spread on the social media site about what George had done when he tackled the terrorists. He himself hadn't logged onto the site since before he stayed at his sister's house in the countryside. The President of the United States Mark Zoola became very tired and frustrated with British politics and at just how slow the opposition parties had been moving to remove the current British government. His advisors briefed him on the current political situation within Britain and how the country and its people would have to vote during the next general election to elect a government and fingers crossed not more of the same. For the Americans it would be a disaster if the British electorate voted to keep the present government in power for a second term of office as it could possibly lead to the destruction of such a great country. Mark could never understand why the country could have ever elected such a government in the first place and one which had turned a great country into a "banana republic" Meanwhile in Poland on an "old" Soviet era Military rifle range a man was firing a sniper's rifle and he was using the Russian made VKS bolt action sniper rifle it fires a supersonic round and housed

172

a silencer it was a perfect rifle and it can bring down a human target even if the person is wearing heavy body armour. He began to fire a few rounds to enable him to zero the rifle, in other words it was having to be adjusted to the user. The telescopic site was adjusted to fire a tight grouping of bullets. A Polish range master was spotting for the man who was using the rifle. The range master thought to himself "this man is no stranger to shooting with a military rifle, he seems to move into position like a trained military man". The range master didn't care who the stranger was just if he was paying him with hard cash for the use of the range privately the stranger paid with US dollars and upfront. The rifle was from the range masters own stock of weapons it wasn't a rifle he normally advertised it was what the stranger had wanted to use and once again he was paying for the privilege he wanted to use a well-known Russian military sniper's rifle fitted with a silencer. The man before him certainly knew all about breathing when taking a shot and not to just snatch at the trigger. After the stranger finished on the range he thought it had felt good to be back on the range and to be practicing with a decent rifle all his previous military training came flooding back to him. Alek travelled to Poland using his European Union passport as such his entry into Poland had gone without any hitches. The next port of call was to Lithuania and onwards to Latvia, the Baltic states were tiny in size compared to countries such as Germany or Poland. Because he was travelling on his European passport it did not pose any problems moving from Lithuania and then onto Latvia. He remained in Latvia for a week where he had spent time planning his next plan of action to travel into Russia. If he did decide to travel to Russia on his European passport he would need to obtain a visa. He did not possess a Russian passport but instead an associate working in Riga the capital of Latvia was working on obtaining a Russian

Caught

passport for him. It was all very cloak and dagger stuff very much the like the cold war period.

By this time over in the UK George along with his sister and his Niece Caitlin accompanied him to Buckingham Palace and his brother in law Dave declined the kind offer to attend as he was very busy at work, his daughter was in awe of her brave uncle. Those who having been awarded an honour or an award in Buckingham Palace could only bring two people as guests. George looked very smart and his award was to be presented to him by none other than the Queen herself. It was a great honour for him. He could not contain his happiness and he was wearing such a big grin on his face his sister could see him smiling from where she was sat she was bubbling over with so much pride. His smile was almost as broad as the joker in the Batman series. Mary's husband said to her before she left for the Palace "as soon as it is all over with bring George back to our house". After the ceremony all three travelled back to the village from London and when they arrived Dave opened the door to the house he shook Georges hand as they walked indoors. George sat down, and opened the box containing the George Cross. Dave asked to look at the medal he handed the medal box over to him and Dave said "George well done you deserve it" Caitlin looked at the medal and then looked at her dad and she said "oh dad it was so wonderful to see uncle George get his medal from the Queen" Mary welled up with tears and said "oh George" Dave spoke up and said "right George we have all been invited to the pub there are some people who wish to meet you". All four walked up the hill towards the pub. They opened the front door to the pub and it brought back so many memories for George. It took him back to that horrible night when the terrorists were killing the people stood around

174

the bar area. As he walked into the bar area he could see the pub was newly decorated. As he approached the bar area the visions of those poor people who were slumped in front of him came flooding back to him and he could still see the blood and parts of brain matter covering the mirror. He stopped inside the pub to take a deep breath the bar was thronging with so many people to the left a buffet was laid out on a table. George spoke first "oh I think we have walked into a private function". Dave said, "yes, it is all for you". It was then that he noticed the man who had backed up what he said to the police when they arrested him on that fateful night. It was the barrister and he approached George and said, "thanks and congratulations you deserve your award". Many drinks later some of the people gathered asked if they could look at his medal. He told them he hadn't brought the medal along with him and he went on to explain he wasn't one to "show off" it was then that Caitlin said, "oh uncle George I have it with me is it OK, I am so sorry". He laughed and said, "of course it is sweetheart" and with that she showed the others her uncles well earnt medal. She was ever so proud of her uncle and what he selflessly did on that fateful night. Many people approached him during the evening and they thanked him for what he did on that awful evening. If it hadn't been for Caitlin, he would never have "shown off" his George Cross as it wasn't his thing to "show off" his motto in life was actions are stronger than mere words. In this case the people of the village and the surrounding areas had wanted to show their appreciation and to thank him for his selfless act. For George to allow his medal to be shown had given some satisfaction for those gathered having known such a brave man had been recognised for his bravery and selfishness when confronting the terrorists who then went on to change so many people's lives. Their lives would never be the same again. For George having been awarded the George Cross had gone some way to help heal their scars of the recent past. In and around the country there were so many villages who were affected by the terrorist attacks. The whole of the country was affected by the events of that day. The terrorist events went such a long way to also help to bring down the government from power. Britain was in a very bad way in some people's eyes the country was deliberately being destroyed by the government and it would take many years to rebuild because of the damage done by the reckless government. One of the more obvious things to do was to get the Americans to lift the food embargo and for NATO to also withdraw the naval blockade from around the United Kingdom. Everything would hinge around the upcoming general election and for the people of Great Britain to decide their future at the ballet box. The President of the USA wanted to be kept informed of everything to do with the UK including the general election, it was top priority. Mark Zoola made his mind up if the people of the UK eventually came to their senses he would immediately lift the food embargo. His political advisors had kept reminding the President the UK isn't like the US. The US was run a little somewhat like a corporate boardroom.

In Paris the city's gendarme were given a tip off regarding a man who hadn't been seen in or around his flat for many weeks, his neighbour who had reported the man as being missing said it was unusual for him to be away from his flat for a such a long time. For the police it was just a normal routine call, the police within the sprawling metropolis would receive hundreds of similar calls each month. The flat where the missing man lived was situated in the old quarter of the city, Le Marais, the flat was situated in large building that was sub divided into six individual flats with two flats on three floors. The flat they were to check on was on the second-floor it was flat number three. Two gendarmes were sent to investigate the supposedly missing occupant and they were expecting to find the occupant in his flat possibly having died from old age. A female and a male policeman were soon deployed to investigate the report. The first thing they did was to check on the neighbours they started at number one and found the occupants were in fact the ones who reported their neighbour as missing. An old man opened the front door and he saw the police officers standing at the door and he invited the two officers inside the flat, where he introduced the police officers to his wife. She explained about their neighbour upstairs and told them he normally kept himself to himself, but he held some far-right political views, the policewoman was slightly taken aback, and asked the lady why she thought that of him. The woman said "well whenever I stuck posters of "Les Republicans" Frances equivalent to the conservative party he would tear down the posters during various elections and he would replace them with material from the National Front, FN. The policeman said, "ah I see". The old man in the flat gave the police the name of the man upstairs, the policewoman stepped outside of the flat and spoke into her radio to make contact with other officers at their police station she asked the person in the station to check on the man living in flat three she wanted to check the man's name the old lady had supplied the police with and the man's name it was "Sacha Laurent" she remained outside of the old couples flat to wait for a response to her request regarding the missing neighbour. The response came through from the station and she was shocked to say the least by the stations update. There had only been 10 people with the same name provided by the old woman, all registered in Paris 2 lived overseas and weren't registered as ever visiting France for almost 8 years. 6 people were old age pensioners and over the age of 80 and 2 died over 2

Caught

years ago at the age of a 100. 2 died at birth, one died 80 years ago and one 35 years ago. The policewoman stepped back inside the flat and asked her colleague to step outside just for a moment. He asked the occupants of the flat to excuse him. As he stepped outside and asked his partner what was going on she explained about the information passed on to her, by the operator at their police station. He said "ok we need to be extremely careful entering the flat upstairs, the missing person is someone who seems to have used someone else's identity. His partner in crime said, "but it's only a missing persons case, I think the only thing we have to be very careful about is if we have to break into the flat".

They were stood outside the man's flat the policeman knocked on the heavy wooden front door he shouted out the man's name, but to no avail there weren't any sounds of movement from inside. He then turned to his colleague "I need to pop to the car and bring the battering ram to break down the door". She replied, "ok but be quick as I want to get back to the station soon so don't piss around getting this bloody door open". He was quick, and he had hold of the hand held, battering ram. He aimed the device at the lock area of the door it took him five very hard hits at the lock eventually he heard the lock mechanism eventually break. They both put their shoulders to the door to force it open it would also be the very last thing they would do on this earth. As soon as they pushed at the door unknown to them the door was booby trapped. The booby trap was put together by a professional someone who knew exactly what they were doing. The booby trap was made up of both Napalm and explosives as the main door was pushed open the police officer's actions set off two explosive devices and the policewoman was covered from head to foot in flaming Napalm she just about managed to get herself up from the floor with all her strength, with her skin on fire she managed to run screaming down the stairs and out into the street where she collapsed in a ball of flames she was eventually subdued by the fire the sight, playing out in the street, was horrific to say the least she burnt to death and her screams were so awful and in her death throes she managed to raise a hand and thrust it skywards it was the last throws of her hideous death. Her colleague inside of the flat was also hit by the Napalm he was covered in flames he also took the full forces of the explosive charge into his stomach he died instantly and there was nothing that could be done for him. Unknown to the pair when entering the flat a laser beam had been inadvertently broken by one of the unsuspecting officers as the pair were unaware of the laser beam. The significance of the beam having been broken was by the breaking of the beam then set off many of the explosive booby traps which were contained within the flat including three more Napalm devices hidden inside the main bedroom. Whoever set up the booby traps used laser beam technology rather than using the old-fashioned method of booby traps by using cord or wire. The main bedroom was where a body was laying undisturbed on top of the bed not under the bed covers the body was fully dressed. It was a male and the body was covered in blood the whoever it was on the bed had a large ugly cut across their throat. Before the flat was covered in flames it there was a body lying in a somewhat backwards motion the position of the head was such the cut across the person's throat was opened much wider and it looked as though someone tried to decapitate the body. Suddenly just as the laser beam was broken by the police officers who unwittingly accessed the flat, the various Napalm devices suddenly ignited inside of the bedroom and covered the room in highly inflammable fuel the flames were intense, and the bed was covered in Napalm and the fire swamped the Napalm. Suddenly several explosives had been detonated and the explosions were destructive they caused part of the flat above to collapse and the debris cascaded into flat below. Luckily no one was at home at the time and part of the debris covered the flat below, whoever constructed the booby traps knew exactly what they were doing. The police, ambulance service and the Paris firefighters were quickly on the scene along with the police bomb squad. The bomb squad and two of the firemen managed to access part of the flat they could just make out what was left of the policeman's body and it was not a pretty sight, covering his legs was a very large slab of concrete debris from the flat above, the bomb squad and the firemen knew there was nothing anyone could do for him it was far too late and besides he was charred beyond all recognition. The fireman extinguished the many flames including the fire around the front door to enable the bomb squad to search for more bombs they soon gave the all clear and entered the kitchen and then the bathroom they soon pronounced the flat was clear it only left the main bedroom to search to dampen down any more fires. Inside the room the bed was also covered in debris from the flat above, they could just make out the shape of another body lying on top of the bed and it was very badly charred, it was beyond all recognition and besides 4 Napalm devices had gone off inside the room and the fire brigade finally extinguished the last of the fires the bomb squad checked the room and confirmed there weren't any more explosives to be found in the bedroom room. The head of the bomb squad reported his findings to the Police Commandant who was leading the investigation he confirmed there weren't any more explosives inside the flat, he would need some time for his team to remove what was left of the various devices found in the flat, the time would allow his team to collect every piece of evidence in situ for his team to then investigate the explosives and the surrounding debris back at their base. The commandant said, "yes that's fine but could you please be quick" the bomb squad officer returned to the flat and an hour or so later he returned to confirm with the commandant the flat was now safe enough to send in his men. The commandant asked the head of the fire detachment to dampen down the flat because the police needed pick through the evidence. They both knew that there wouldn't be too much to go on because the fire had wreaked so much damage also the water damage due to the extinguishing of the various fires. A young fireman jumped from his fire truck and the first thing he came across was the once young police officer as he looked at her body he was sick it was due to her body having been burnt to a cinder it wasn't a nice sight even to a seasoned emergency operator. Someone from the ambulance team wanted to give the police officer some dignity and away from the prying eyes there where by now many photographers who by had gathered outside the flat, even so most press photographers have very long-range lenses on their cameras and could take a picture from a great distance. The Chief fire officer reported to the Police Commandant "Sir I have just been into the flat I can tell you from my experience my nose tells me some form of Napalm and explosives has been used to destroy the flat, I can just make out a body at the front door and I am afraid to tell you it is one of your officers, I am so sorry". The Police Commandant thanked the fire chief. It was now just a waiting game to fully access the crime scene and get forensics inside and for them to carry out their work he will have to arrange the recovery of his officer and to begin to put the many jigsaw pieces together and to investigate the stranger found inside the flat. Meanwhile the police woman was photographed by forensics and she was still in the grotesque position where she fell. The Commandant had given permission as soon as the forensic team were finished for her body to be then removed from the crime scene. A coroner's van was parked nearby, and the coroner's team eventually took her body away with as much dignity as they could. Meanwhile upstairs on the stairs the forensic team found the battering ram used by their colleagues to gain access to the flat. The battering ram was dropped on the stair well, forensics took many photographs and of course of the front door including the surrounding area. The fire brigades own fire forensics team investigated the burn marks on the wall and over the stair well the fire was so ferocious and the Napalm covering the police woman spewed onto the stairs as she ran covering in the stuff. They entered the flat to begin the examine of the policeman's body once his body had been photographed and forensically searched and the scene documented the Commandant was able to give permission to remove his body from the flat. He could see the damage indicating the ferocity of the fire. He could see his two officers had not stood a chance entering the booby trapped flat. As the remains of the policeman were carried from the building and into the coroner's vehicle all the emergency services outside in the street stopped what they were doing and they all bowed their heads in respect to the fallen policeman. The forensics team and fire brigade entered the main bedroom and began to photograph and record the scene inside the room and once the fire and the intense heat subsided the body in the bed was burnt to a crisp and due to some masonry having fallen from the ceiling and from the flat above it then fell onto the bed in the flat below and parts of the body in the bed hadn't burnt so much as the rest of the body. One of the bodies hands wasn't as badly burnt it was partially due to pieces of masonry having covered the hand the deceased's head was burnt beyond all recognition. The forensic team and members of the coroner's office had to be extremely careful when recovering what remained of the body on the bed the only way to remove it was to fetch a rubber body bag into the bedroom to then try their very best to keep the body intact without it crumbling to pieces once they were ready to remove it from the flat. When the team had attempted to lift the remains, much of the body disintegrated into ash. One of the forensic team had a dustpan and brush and he brushed up as much of the blackened and charred pieces of the body to then place the ash into the body bag, it took almost an hour to get most of what remained of the body into the body bag. The flat threw up one surprise after another. In the main bedroom inside a wardrobe there were the remains of two AK 47 Assault Rifles and a pistol. Inside the kitchen and inside one of the store cupboards when looking inside the police could see it contained so much ammunition and the cupboard was at bursting point the ammunition was neatly piled up in boxes, the cupboard looked just like a storeroom in an armoury. Inside the living room there was what was left of a cardboard box inside the box there were the burnt remnants of a couple of passports. Found under the bed was lots of pieces of burnt money and there must have been thousands of Euros. The evidence found inside the flat was soon gathered up for further examination back at the Police Station. The owner of the block of flats was contacted and he was asked to visit the station for further questioning he was told to bring all the paper work he had on the person who was renting flat number three. The landlord duly arrived at the police station and the following morning with all the paper work he had on the man and it was the first time there was a name of the man who was living at the flat, but it was the same name given by the old couple at flat one. As soon as the landlord made his statement to the police and handed over all the documentation, including a copy of the man's passport confirming his name was indeed that of

Caught

"Sacha Laurent", the police's initial check of the name used was false and so the passport must have been a forgery. The landlord was free to leave the station, he carried out every procedure required of a landlord when renting accommodation in France. A day later the police realised just before the police woman was murdered she was checking on the name the old couple had given her regarding the man who was living in flat number 3. The police woman serving in the control room on that fateful day confirmed she was indeed passed on information to the officer regarding the name check. The documentation from the landlord passed to the police reflected it was the same man who was renting the flat his bank account, provided to the landlord, was legitimate, it was the same account which was used to pay the rent each month there was one thing which seemed peculiar and it was twenty fours before his rent was due to be paid and a lot of money had been placed into his account from an off-shore account. The police tried to trace where the money was transferred from, but the off-shore account had been closed two days prior to the flat being blown to pieces. The forensic team leader and the senior detective investigating the murders were summoned to the police commandant's office. As they sat down he said, "gentlemen who ever blew up the flat is a professional and with military combat experience". He went on to explain the French secret service wanted to take over the investigation, but they had been fobbed off for now. The forensic team along with the coroner managed to extract some DNA and a partial finger print off the body found in the flat. On further investigation, it was confirmed the body was that of a male and the forensic team had found before the man was burnt to a crisp and his throat was cut wide open to the bone and he was almost decapitated by what seemed like some form of hunting knife the blade cut through the skin like a knife cutting through butter, the cutting motion was stopped by the knife cutting into the man's spine. When the coroner carried out an autopsy he could make out a deep cut into the man's spinal column. On one of the hands which was not severely burnt both the coroner and the forensic team managed to lift a partial print. The commandant told the head of forensics to get his finger out from his arse and put the prints and the DNA through the INTERPOL, The International Crime Police Organization, database. The Commandant already knew from the evidence gathered indicated the perpetrator was someone who had military experience whoever it was were determined to burn the flat to a cinder and to destroy any evidence or clues to what was going inside the Paris flat. The passports found at the flat, as far as the police could make out were Russian and American. The scraps of money were Russian Rubble, Ukrainian Hryvnia, Euros and British Pounds. The two AK47 assault rifles and the pistol were found to have their serial numbers erased using acid. The ammunition was found to come from the Russian Military. The coroner informed the Commandant the man found inside the flat was dead long before the flat was fire bombed. The two police officers entering the flat were burnt to death by Napalm booby trap devices. The person who booby trapped the building and rigged up the devices to an intricate laser system setting off the booby traps in the flat ensuring maximum affect. 24 hours later the head of forensics came to see the Commandant and as he walked into his office the commandant was finishing off a cigarette. "Ah Bernard what do you have for me today"? The officer replied, "Victor you will not believe me when I tell you what I have found". The Commandant replied, "you mean to tell me you have at last found out something about the mysterious body found in the flat"? Bernard replied "yep let me try and explain the man was not Sacha Laurent? INTERPOL have his finger prints and DNA on their files as a Sage Vasiliev he was caught trying to purchase some high velocity rifles in Poland so when we ran his DNA through various databases his DNA profile turned up on a Ukrainian database, Ukraine which has only recently opened to the rest of the world and were only recently sharing data with Europe as they are desperately trying to be accepted as a new nation joining the European Union. "But Victor it came back as a bloody Major Alek Petrov having served with the Russian special forces and he was apparently killed in the Ukraine when the Russian backed forces clashed with Ukrainian troops"!! Victor slowly replied, "fuck, what is a bloody supposedly dead Russian soldier doing years later, dead in a bloody Parisian flat for Christ sake" The Commandant knew the case was not all it had first seemed. Something bigger was afoot. Meanwhile the funeral of the two police officers had recently taken place and many dignitaries attended the funerals there were many plaudits paid to the memory of the two officers' including mention of their loyal service to the citizens of Paris.

Meanwhile in Britain the government tried its best to persuade the public to vote for a second term of office and to have more of the same politics from the Marxist leftist government. The incident in Paris barely got a mention in the British press the American president Mark Zoola could have so easily have lifted the food embargo on Britain and he could have also persuaded NATO to lift the Naval blockade, that is if he wanted to. But he wasn't going to do anything about the blockades because the current British government could have used the lifting of both blockades for its own political agenda. The President wanted to wait for the outcome of the upcoming British elections before showing his hand. Events in the world were moving too quickly, for people to understand what was happening. Long gone were the days when the world moved at a much slower pace. Events in Britain were a prime example of how events changed too much and in such a short space of time, as always it was the ordinary people who suffer in the end. Politicians never seem to grasp how ordinary people always ended up being the casualties of failed governments and left with the consequences of failed policies. Within three and half years the government of the day had virtually bankrupted the country and ended up angering the President of the United States so much, so he authorised the food blockade and NATO to place a Naval blockade around the coast of Great Britain and it happened in such a short space of time.

Meanwhile the Ukrainian authorities were open in recording the death of the Russian officer Major Alek Petrov it seemed to have the hall marks of a James Bond film. Alek Petrov having initially been, captured in a fire fight between Russian and Ukrainian forces. He was then due to be shot by firing squad and at the very last minute he was reprieved. One reason for his reprieve was he was far more use to the Ukrainians alive. Under interrogation his captors soon concluded Alek was not so keen on the Russians after all they found his mother came from the Russian Caucasus region her village was burnt to the ground by Russian forces at the time she was a teenager and against all odds she managed to travel to Moscow where she subsequently met Alek's father and they later married and had two children, both boys. Alek's brother Dimitri joined the Russian Army and he was killed while he served in Afghanistan, he would not be the last soldier killed in action within the country. Decades later many more soldiers would be killed and so many ended up severely maimed and damaged in one way or another. Many soldiers from the far flung reaches of the world would end up dead in so many wars and conflicts across the world mothers would continue to shed many tears. Alek formed a deep-rooted hatred for Russia and his sympathies lay with the people of the Caucasus. His mother would tell him stories about her family and her ancestors. The men of the Caucasus are proud fighter's a warrior race. Hence when Alek was old enough he decided to join the Russian Army he showed great leadership and courage he was soon selected for training in the Spetsnaz, it was an elite force just like many of the European special forces. Today the Russian press prefer to refer to the elite group as SOBR, Alpha and Vityaz. Alek successfully completed the special forces it was tough and extremely rigorous training. He steadily rose through the ranks to the rank of Major. During the Russian Ukraine conflict, he soon found an opportunity to enable him to disappear from his lines and hence how easily it was for the Ukrainian forces to capture him and alive? During his captivity he slowly revealed the hatred he held for Russia and indeed his need to revenge his relatives killed in the Caucasus by the Russian military many years earlier. After the Ukrainians rescinded his death by firing squad the military moved Alek to Kiev, the capital of the Ukraine where they eventually handed him over to the SBU, the Security Services of Ukraine. They interrogated him for weeks on end and they found his story held out during his interrogation a member of the SBU infiltrated the area of the Caucasus where Alek's mother's village had once stood his story was found to be true. In Moscow another SBU agent was checking on Aleks Russian family and they found the information he provided regarding his brother's death in Afghanistan serving with the Russian Army was also true regarding his father having taken his own life because of the news of his son's death, Alek's beloved mother died a few years ago. His story stood up to the rigorous investigation and the

Ukrainians were happy to allow him to live. A secret agent also managed to access Alek's Russian military records and his military service had also proved to be true. In Kiev Alek was suddenly a person of interest to the SBU and to some people on the fringes of government they all found him of great interest a person who might at some time in the future be able to assist some government officials who worked in the shadows of government. Some of the security services in the Ukraine thought they could use him as a lone wolf to help turn his hatred of the Russians for their own use.

Alek's DNA was recorded on a Russian military database hence why it was, when the French police ran the DNA of the dead man found in the Paris flat, through the Russian police's database his DNA was matched with the blood the forensic team in Paris recovered from his supposedly charred body, unknown to everyone connected to the Paris attacks the body found in the flat had laid on the bed for many weeks previously to throw the French security services off track, the Ukrainian secret service had already taken the man's DNA when he was based in the Ukraine and then manipulated the real Alek Petrov's military data along with his DNA and replaced his data with the man who was found in the Parisian flat, they also managed to manipulate the Russian military's database to reflect the same data held on the Ukrainian military database. As mentioned after many months of having been held in captivity and under intense interrogation after the secret service had received the reports from their SBU agents who were sent to Russia to check Alek's story of his home life and his military service the SBU soon came up with a plan they decided to turn him into a double agent as he was already highly trained due to his Russian special forces intense training. He was taught by the SBU to become a secret agent he learnt all about how to operate as a spy. It was soon recognised that he was an excellent shot he was given more training as a sniper he was a natural. The Ukrainians came up with a plan and it was a very ambitious plan. After his training and another change of name he was issued with a French European passport, he spoke many languages and French was a language he excelled at. The SBU facilitated his journey into France and they paid for his flat he was also paid a regular wage and he also received bonuses to carry out work for his masters. Eventually East European weapons and munitions were smuggled into France. Alek was given a French name Martin Montage, there was so much subterfuge being played out also behind the scenes. The man killed in the flat was not who he had seemed when his DNA was run through the DNA databases it was matched to the DNA held on the Ukrainian police database and it returned the DNA for a Major Alek Petrov. But the real Major Alek Petrov was still alive and breathing he was supposedly the man who was murdered in Paris but after the destruction of the flat he was moved immediately out of France he was in fact heading further East and was to be used in a much more daring plot. Lurking in the background was a more ruthless agent who was about to enter the fray he was called Dmytro. Back in Paris Victor said to Bernard "I think we may have a spy or an espionage ring, with a professional killer on our hands we may have to dig around in some very dark corners of the underworld". Bernard agreed with his colleague and he left the office to carry on with the investigation. While Victor was sat in his office his telephone rang when he spoke it was his boss the Perfect for the district of Paris. Victor sat straight and kept saying "yes sir, certainly sir". After the call he placed the phone onto its cradle and he realised his boss was under pressure possibly placed on him by the

Minister of the Interior. During the same afternoon Victor received an email from Bernard informing him the dead man's bank accounts were now closed, and the account overseas has suddenly disappeared, and the details of all the man's bank accounts are blocked. Victor thanked him for the update. He sat at his desk and while he was contemplating what the hell was going he suddenly had a gut feeling another country's secret service might be somehow involved in the dead man's demise, it had the feel of a secret service organisation was operating and working in parallel with his investigating. It all stank of someone with military experience and whose grubby bloody hands were all over the firebombing and it certainly wasn't a bunch of amateurs at work. The forensic teams poured over the burnt out flat with a fine-tooth comb their preliminary results set out in the report highlighted the following points. The man found inside the bedroom was killed long before the explosions and the Napalm devices were eventually set off. His throat had been cut with a single motion and had been cut with such force that the blade cut straight through the windpipe into the man's spinal column. The dead man, Sage Vasiliev, must have known his assailant because apart from the booby-trapped doors it was found the front door was locked from the inside and there hadn't been a struggle it looked like the victim knew the assailant and let him enter the flat. The perpetrator and this is where the plot thickens the man who escaped was a double agent he left the flat via the fire escape that runs down the side of the building. Whoever set up the lasers and the booby traps knew exactly what they were doing and whoever it is has been highly trained and they knew exactly what they were doing and just possibly is a trained assassin. The Napalm and the explosives were of a military grade and from a Russian factory. The forensics team did not find a single serial number on the rifles or on the pistol.

Caught

Many armies in the world were issued with the AK47 Rifle. The only good news was regarding the ammunition because on the base of every round of ammunition are various markings and the markings can be traced to the country producing the ammunition. Bernard was only able to trace it to either Russia or the Ukraine region, it could only be traced to the two countries as at one time the country's, were once governed by the Soviet Union, during the soviet era the munitions were still in use by both countries. The money found in the flat could not be traced. The passports were reported stolen from various European countries the people who had their passports stolen were visiting tourists. The passports recovered in the flat were found to have been cancelled by the tourists via their own country's embassies. Alek may have been a supply man or quartermaster and was perhaps helping to supply agents who were based in Paris. Victor could not work out why there had been so much effort used to destroy the flat because for him it seemed too much of an overkill. His thoughts were n ow focused on his fallen officers and their families. Whoever booby trapped the flat must have known the police would have eventually been called to investigate the whereabouts of the man found in flat No 3. Victor was trying very hard to work out why a Russian soldier supposedly reported as having been killed in action in the Ukraine and then ends up being murdered in some Parisian flat many years after his supposed death. So far nothing regarding the case was making any sense to him.

Meanwhile in Riga Francois was met by a Russian man who was sent to drive him to Russia. Francois needed a permit issued by the Russian FSB department as the border region is a restricted region and is referred to as the border security zone of Russia.

He could have travelled to the International Border Transit Point but instead he really wanted to travel through the security zone. His paper work was finally issued even though he was by now travelling on a Russian passport. Once again, he was travelling under a different name and this time he was to be known as Alexei Kozlov a businessman working within the Baltic States. His drivers name was Mikel and it took them several days to travel into the heartland of the Russian state. They were to be based just a few miles outside of Kostroma in a house within a dense forest surrounding the city. François, aka Alek, payed Mikel a handsome reward for taking him to Kostroma. The following morning Mikel left the house to travel and to visit some relatives nearby it would not be suspicious staying in Russia for a few more days, rather than travelling immediately travelling to Riga. A local taxi took François twenty miles to a house just off the beaten track he realised he would need to be extremely careful as there was military school near to where he was staying. The taxi driver was handsomely paid and as he drove away he thought to himself the stranger spoke with a southern Russian accent not heard so much in northern Russia. Alek moved to the area to cover his tracks and all the facilities he required were in place for him to use. The following day there was a knock at the door and he very carefully opened the door with a pistol in his hand. The stranger standing at the front door spoke "oh Alek that's no way to greet a fellow countryman". He replied, "how long have you been in the country, quick get inside before someone see's you" The stranger stepped inside and said, "I have been here a month setting up your safe houses". He walked into the main room a huge fire was blazing away. He spoke "Alek the bloody SBU took a while to make sure everything was in place for me to get into this god forsaken country" He looked around the room and turned to Alek "blimey you did a bloody good job in

Caught

Paris, poor old Sacha, bloody Russian". He replied "yes I had to eradicate Sacha he was putting two and two together and he knew he was being used by the SBU and very soon our masters found out that he also had a lucrative deal on the side line he was selling weapons to gangsters and known terrorist it would not have been too long before the French police found out what he was up to and so he was liquidated" Dmytro replied "yes the department thought as much, so now let us talk about tomorrow we should be able to collect the VKS sniper rifle with the built in silencer". Alek said, "yes I have already fired one in Poland and it will do the job". His colleague spoke "I have found a hunter's range further into the forest it is perfect, I have arranged for no one working at the ranges to be around and they have all been paid off to keep their mouths shut tight". The pair had a good night's sleep and the following morning they ate a hearty breakfast to set them up for a very long day and while Alek was busying himself in Russia. The police in Paris were erring on the side of caution regarding the body found in the flat and the deaths of their fellow comrades it was a dirty case of espionage being played out on the streets of Paris. The police commandant was extremely concerned about the possibility of so many automatic weapons finding their way into the hands of criminals. So, he decided to visit the prefect of Paris, he wanted to get permission to flood an area of Paris with both police and soldiers to help to flush out any known terrorists and their sympathisers, hopefully at the same time flushing out any hardened criminals and to cordon off a search area so those who escaped the cordon would be arrested by troops who would help to surround the area. The prefect agreed with Victor's plan of action and authorised the searches. The area selected to be searched was a notorious gangland area of Paris some of the occupants thought they were immune from the police. The searches began at four in the morning by the end of the searches 20 people were arrested during the raids most of those arrested attempted to get past the military cordon. The police recovered ten assault rifles and five pistols. At the central police station ten people were released without charge it was soon established they only ran from the area because seven of the men were having affairs and three women informed their husbands they were staying overnight with girlfriends when in fact they were staying overnight at their boyfriend's flats. Victor didn't want to get too bogged down with minor issues in fact they hadn't committed any criminal acts. He got his teams to verify their stories and once each of their stories were verified they were released from custody and nothing further was ever said. It was the remaining ten people he was most interested in. Bernard's forensic team were checking the rifles and they found 10 rifles only 8 were missing their serial numbers having been removed by using acid. A similar method used on the rifles and pistols found inside the burnt out flat. 2 of rifles were found in a well-known gangster's flat and a pistol was also found at the same flat. The rifles and pistol were traced to Poland the details were soon passed onto the Polish authorities. The gangsters were charged with possessing unauthorised firearms. Victor was happy with the results of the raids and he had 8 rifles previously unaccounted for and 4 pistols off the streets of Paris. He suspected the weapons were supplied by the man found dead at the Parisian flat. The forensic team managed to identify those arrested and cross referenced the rifles with their finger prints. The ballistics teams examined and fired the weapons in the underground range at the police building and cross referenced the distinctive markings on each bullet fired from the rifles to see if any were used in previous crimes. They found 2 rifles were used in armed robberies and the men found in possession of the rifles while searching their flats were duly charged with various serious firearm offences. On a few of the rifles there were some partial prints they were matched to the dead man found in the flat, one of his hands had some finger prints intact. The weapons found during the police raids were heavy assault rifles along with the pistols they were found to be of East European military issue. There was another set of fingers prints they were confirmed as the Russian Alek Petrov alias Francois, the police still did not realise his actual name was in fact Alek Petrov. The link was eventually made to the burnt out flat, but for Victor and his police department they managed to take off the Paris streets a substantial amount of high calibre weaponry and ammunition. Bernard submitted his forensic report regarding the weapons and he added the forensic evidence to the report. The ammunition found during the raids was the same batch found in the flat where the body was found. All routes were leading the investigation toward the East to possibly to Russia or the Ukraine. Victor read the reports submitted by the various police teams and it was for him to collate the data and to formulate a single report to try and make some sense of it. He quite rightly concluded the Paris police had indeed uncovered a spy and possibly a logistics cell operating out of the Paris flat. For some reason one of the spies was murdered by a member of the same spy ring and whoever the person or persons were, they tried desperately to eradicate the evidence within the flat by burning it. He concluded the man who was found in the flat was cynically killed because he may have known far too much about the spy ring? The "second" agent had booby trapped the flat and escaped from the building via the fire escape hence why the front door was locked from the inside, the two police officers did not check the rear of the house presumably because they thought it was just a routine visit and to possibly find a lonely old person dead inside the flat. He submitted his report to his boss who would have to eventually having added his comments to the document to then submit Victors report to the Minister of the Interior. The Minister was sat in his office reading the commandants extremely in-depth report regarding the recent murders in Paris. He concluded there was at least two other countries secret service agents openly operating within the city. His conclusion was he could not see anyone ever being held to account over the murders, he sat with heavy heart knowing full well his conclusions would upset many people. He would also be recommending to the French Prime Minister to write a very stern letter to both the Russian Ambassador to France and the Ukrainian Ambassador. A week after Victor submitted his findings a message filtered down to him from high up in government circles and well above his own pay grade informing him that the case was to be closed and was now out of his hands. Victor wasn't surprised by the conclusions of the report. He gathered everyone together who was involved in the murder investigation and as they gathered in the main office he began by thanking them for their valiant efforts in attempting to solve the case. He finally told them the case would be wound up and sadly closed. After the group heard his last sentence suddenly there were many raised voices "no it can't be surely" he replied, "I am so sorry I have to say is the case is out of my hands all I can say it was due to our initial Police team stumbling into was now known as an espionage case I am afraid the culprit or culprits would be by now long gone" and with that he left the office. It left a very bad taste in his throat and he was angry, at the way the case was ended. He knew the case was ingrained in the dark and murky world of espionage and spies where no one could trust the person next to them. There was a knock-on effect because of the two Ambassadors having received the diplomatic letters of complaint written by the French Prime Minister. Normally in diplomatic terms a Prime Minister would invite another country's Ambassador to his official office and to formally hand an Ambassador a letter of protest in person. In this case the Prime Minister was extremely angry he did not think it was fitting to hand the letters personally and it was a snub to both Ambassadors and they knew it. The letters had ramifications in Eastern Europe first, the Russian Ambassador contacted his countries Prime Minister Vladimir Soholov in Moscow, who told the Ambassador to open the envelope and read the contents to him over the phone. He stopped the Ambassador in mid sentence and told him to send a copy of the letter via the secure link he explained he would need to brief Mr President. The Ambassador put the phone down and he summoned his FSB senior officer "Alex send this letter to the prime minister's office right now. Do not make a copy and return the letter to me as soon as you have confirmed with Moscow they have received the letter. He replied, "yes Mr Ambassador". Inside the Ukrainian Embassy the Ambassador read the French Prime Ministers letter he thought to himself "bloody hell, what are the SBU up to now"? At the time the Ukraine was attempting to get its house to enable the country to join the European Union and it did not want an espionage incident to suddenly blow up in the governments face and for the incident to be linked to the Ukrainian government. The ambassador spoke directly to the president he asked for a copy of the letter to be sent to his office via the secure link. The Ambassador personally sent the letter. In Moscow the Prime Minister had by now received the copy of the letter as he sat reading the contents he called for a meeting with his security ministers. Meanwhile Alek was on the rifle range and deep inside a forest not too far away from Moscow his colleague was stood next to him holding a pair of binoculars he was spotting for Alek. The snipers rifle was delivered to the range by "the armourer" the rifle was to be used for his latest assignment. The pair had in their possession an abundance of ammunition and they stayed at the range for most of the day. Alek needed to zero the rifle he also needed to be comfortable handling it and he practiced stripping the rifle apart and putting it together again until it became second nature for him. He said "Dmytro we are finished here my friend". It was high time to return to the house before it gets any darker. The range staff were handsomely paid to clean the range up and to pick up the used brass casings. The ammunition was of a Russian make and as such would not alert anyone to what recently took place at the range.

In Britain the general election race was gathering pace. Each party were out on the ground canvassing for the publics vote the main parties travelled the length and breadth of the country. It looked as though there would be a high percentage turn out on voting day. The prime minister Julien Jones knew his governments time would be up. He would go down in history as the prime minister who almost brought the country crashing to its knees almost destroying the country. The opposition coalition were at last a formidable opposition within Parliament. On the day of the election the voter only had two options open to them vote for the same government and policies or vote a new government into power. That evening after the people voted the initial exit polls seemed to be predicting the government of Julien Jones would stay in power. The following morning votes were still being counted and the results known to the public and it looked as though the opposition were romping home with a landslide win. By late morning Julien Jones and his party had indeed lost the election by a mile it was a landslide victory for the opposition the government were humiliated at the ballot box, proving the people were very disillusioned at his government and everything they stood for. In Ukraine the president called the head of the SBU to his office. When the head eventually turned up the President handed him a copy of the French Prime Ministers letter. The President demanded to know what the hell was going on and what did the director think he was playing at? He replied, "I don't know please let me contact my office"? The President replied, "leave my office now and be back here within the hour and with some answers". The man left the office and travelled back to the SBU headquarters. At the same time in Russia Alek made himself ready for the task at hand. He and Dmytro were sat in a 4X4 vehicle it was the same one used to bring them to the ranges. The vehicle was configured to smuggle weapons it was easy to conceal weapons in the vehicle. The pair had a five and half hour journey ahead of them from Kostroma to Moscow it was a very early start. On the drive to the target Alek drove first and then he slept when his colleague took over the driving. They arrived in the outskirts of Moscow by ten thirty in the morning just before the pair left the safe house an SBU agent gave them the details of the target and where the target was known to be over the following 48 hours. In Kiev the head of the SBU was briefing the president on his agent's mission inside of Russia. The president was furious he ordered the head of the SBU to cancel the operation or eradicate his agent immediately he didn't care what he had to do but just cancel the operation. The head of the SBU told the president it was impossible to carry out his order because the agents were by now out of contact as per operational instructions. Unknown to anyone in Kiev Dmytro kept hold of a backup mobile phone and he was totally disobeying his boss's strict instructions. Whilst they were in Moscow the pair were starving and so Alek jumped out of the vehicle to purchase a McDonalds breakfast for the pair. Dmytro took a quick look at his phone he could see there was a missed text message. It read "Abort and destroy all evidence" he pulled a pistol that was concealed inside of his jacket and as soon as Alek sat in the passenger seat and buckled himself in he was about to hand a breakfast to his colleague but it was then that he noticed the pistol and before he could say anything Dmytro pulled the trigger on the pistol and shot Alek in the stomach, the pistol was fitted with a silencer the scene inside of the vehicle was ironic because one assassin took out another. He shot Alek in the side of his stomach with a 9mm dumdum round and the mass of fat and stomach muscle helped to slow the bullet down and it remained lodged inside Alek's stomach. There was a large amount of blood covering the seat and Dmytro pulled a blanket off the back seats and he stuffed it into the entry wound. He then placed a baseball cap, and a pair of sunglasses on the body. He then drove back to where he just driven from and with the hope no one had discovered the house. He arrived at the safe house and by now it was dark late in the evening. He hauled Alek's body from the vehicle it was very difficult to get the body from the vehicle and into the house but once inside he threw the body onto a settee. The house was constructed entirely of wood and inside he found a large wooden crate inside was the equipment he would need to finish his task? You see he was the safety valve for the SBU for if things went wrong and he was there to pick up the pieces. Outside the house there was another 4X4 and it was a Range Rover Sport, funny enough the vehicle did not stand out because in and around Moscow there were so many people who also owned high spec western cars. He took a can of petrol from the other 4X4 inside the house he went upstairs and poured petrol over the beds and on the wooden stairs as he walked into the kitchen he splashed some more of the petrol onto the worktops. He then threw the remaining petrol over the body which was still sprawled out on the settee. He then started to rig the house with explosives and Napalm incendiary devices. He only rigged up the one laser beam device it was rigged so it would go off just as soon as the front door was opened. He took another can of petrol from the range rover and soaked the other vehicle in the petrol. The area stank of petrol fumes he moved the Range Rover away from the other vehicle and away from the house. He opened the front door of the house and deliberately set off the Napalm booby traps scattered inside the building. He then approached the 4x4 and threw a match into the vehicle and it soon went up in flames. The whole area was now ablaze, and it was lit up just like the Blackpool illuminations. The light of the flames could be seen for miles he jumped into the Range Rover and drove towards the main highway. He noticed the mileage he could see he had only driven for about 6 kilometres he was just leaving the forest when he heard the first of the explosions, the fuses on the explosives were set with timers. He felt so much better having left the cover of the forest and he drove south towards Belarus from there he would be able to enter the Ukraine without any problems. While he was driving he was listening to the local news he heard the news announcer reporting on an incident within a forest the same one he had recently left. The announcer was reporting a fire and the local emergency services could not reach the fire as they were hindered from accessing the fire because metal tacks were thrown across the access road. Dmytro thought to himself "great it did work" he knew the longer the house burnt the less evidence would be recovered from the burnt-out building. He felt that the rifle left on top of the body would partially melt the serial numbers had been previously burnt off with acid. He eventually arrived at the Russian Belarus border and when he crossed the border he filled the vehicle with fuel he also filled two Jerry cans with petrol. As he paid the young woman at the till she spoke to him and said "nice car" but he didn't reply and paid for the fuel he drove off heading towards central Belarus. Further on he again stopped for more petrol then he headed south for the Ukraine and home. In Russia the wooden house had been burnt to the ground and there wasn't much left inside the building. The body was burnt to a crisp nothing remained of what was until recently a human being. The police knew by just looking at the remains of the powdery outline of the body it was all that was left of someone who not so long ago was alive. On top of the body was the remains of a rifle.

At the same time as the events in Russia. In Britain a new prime minister was elected into power, and the Marxist leftist party had been roundly defeated. As the latest Prime Minister walked into his office at Number 10 Downing Street he had some much-needed good news. The President of America recently phoned him, and he explained he was lifting the food embargo and the NATO naval blockade was going to be lifted. The president was instrumental in granting the new government a fairer lending rate and the IMF also agreed on short term lending rates. The Prime Minister stopped the foreign overseas budget and transferred the billions of pounds into much needed funds and various needy budgets and would immediately benefit the country. He knew he could not justify the aid budget anymore, especially when the country was on the verge of bankruptcy.

In Belarus Dmytro knew that he would have to report to the SBU headquarters in Kiev. But when he arrived in Kiev he was instructed not to approach the Headquarters and instead to take a few days off from work. He was only back in Ukraine for a few days and during this period he was staying with his girlfriend Sasha. She hadn't seen him for a few months she had no idea he was working for the SBU. She despised the SBU and all it stood for, as a student many of her close friends were involved in peaceful protests the SBU and the security service including the civil police arrested many of her student friends and they all disappeared without trace they were more than likely arrested by the SBU or handed over to them by the civil police and they were never seen again. Their families and friends petitioned the government of the day for the students release and not one was ever released. While Dmytro waited to be summoned by the head of his department at the SBU Headquarters he remained at his girlfriend's flat in the centre of Kiev. One morning he received a text form his boss who summoned him "into work". He was prepared for a very long day at the office? That morning he said his goodbyes to Sasha they kissed as he left the flat she thought to herself he had been shaking but she just shrugged off the idea. He drove over to the building where the SBU operated from and he suddenly became very nervous as he did not have a clue what to expect when he eventually met the "boss". He knocked on the large wooden office door someone from inside shouted "enter" Dmytro walked into the palatial looking office, a hangover from the Soviet era and sat behind a large oak table was a tiny man. He said, "ah welcome back I hear you had a very busy time while visiting the "motherland"". He was referring to Russia and not the Ukraine. He replied, "no not really it was a close call who called off the operation and why"? The man behind the desk replied, "the operation was called off by people at the very top of government, ours is not to ask questions but to carry out orders asked of any of us". He replied, "oh I see, so it doesn't matter who is eradicated carrying out those orders then"? the reply was "exactly now just leave it at that". He stood up and walked over to where Dmytro was sat "on this mission we do not need a report in any form the assignment as far as you are concerned never took place". Dmytro looked up at the man and replied, "that's ok my report is in a very safe place let us just call it my insurance policy". His "boss" replied "A man after my own heart and I understand I can assure you that no harm will come to you and that I can promise now I know you have a document and I hope it will protect you". He enquired about Alek's remains his boss replied "the Russian authorities have nothing to go on apart from his cremated body it hadn't given any leads or clues to who he is. The Russian authorities put the unknown persons death down to an inter mob (mafia) murder. The case was soon closed and the head of the SBU was sent a message from the head of the FSB in Moscow. It read "we have found one of your agents in the Kostroma forest. Stay well away from Russia you have been warned so don't dump your rubbish in our territory". It was a straight forward message and very much straight to the point. His boss looked at Dmytro and spoke "young man you have served your country well". He thought to himself "fuck now what is he about to say to, I need to get out of here and soon". His boss continued with his speech "and as such we cannot risk putting you back into the field of operations, the president has authorised me to inform you from here on you are now forthwith retired from the service on a very handsome pension and with a large pay off". He replied, "in other words a payoff" his boss sarcastically replied, "it's better than a bullet in your head or your body and floating down the Dnieper river now do I make myself clear"? He replied, "yes especially when you put it like that" they shook hands his boss spoke "leave your issued pistol at reception on your way out of the building". As he got out of the chair he thought to himself "thank fuck for that it could have gone a lot worse". As he arrived at the reception desk and the man manning the desk spoke as he saw Dmytro arrive "Ahh we have been expecting you comrade, I require you to hand over your issued pistol" Dmytro handed the pistol over to the man and walked out of the building hopefully for the last time. He stepped into the bustling city centre and the sun was out in the bright blue sky. He thought to himself "I will check my bank account to find out if he was true to his word regarding the money". He duly found a branch of his bank and asked the woman behind the till for an up to date account statement. He was required to produce his bank card and some form of ID. The woman soon printed off an account statement. His account was in credit to 7533.27 Ukrainian Hryvnia equivalent to £2000.000 he knew it was only the first lump sum payment as the head of the SBU informed him there would be two more separate payments of equal amounts paid over two months along with the payments would be a monthly pension. So far, he was happy.

In Britain the latest Prime Minister was trying and quickly to reverse some of the previous governments mad decisions. The first thing he had to do was to take down the public statues and to replace the statues with copies as the Prime Minister thought the original statues had been destroyed, not knowing they were in fact safe. The head of public works in the UK asked to meet the Prime Minister as a matter of urgency. The PM asked him to give him a call and he would make time to meet him. The head of public works duly turned up at the prime minister's office at Number 10 Downing Street, he entered the front door and as he approached the front door of No 10 Downing Street the world's press were interviewing the chancellor of the exchequer, the head of public works was filmed entering the building. He entered the PM's office and the Prime Minister stood up to shake the man's hand he then switched off the TV on the wall and he offered the head of public works a seat and a cup of tea he declined the offer and he sat down. The PM asked him what he could do for him and what the man told him made Mark smile from ear to ear. The head of works spoke "Mr prime Minister I am not a person to beat about the bush" he began to explain about the missing and supposedly destroyed, statues and their current location hidden within the Welsh mountains. Mark was lost for words he could not believe what he just heard. The Prime Minister requested a list of everything hidden away and the Prime minister was over the moon at the news. It was such a good start to restoring the country to a better place to live in the country's history goes a long way to help. The head of works left the building he felt venerated in helping to save the icon statues for future generations. The Prime Minister reinstated the UK's delegation to the NATO organisations headquarters as it is a vital link. He would also go on to reinstate the UK as a member of the UN. It would be a dereliction of his duty not to reinstate the UK to both organisations. The American president was soon in contact with the UK's government to enable the UK to progress in the world he wanted to assist the UK in restoring the country to a level not seen prior to the Marxist leftist governments car crash election. It hadn't been too long before the British people began to feel the benefits of the food embargo having been lifted. For many to be able to purchase food denied to them since the embargo was a god send. Things in the country after much effort by the new government and of course the people and by America began to slowly get back to some form of normality. There was something Mark Brown had made a priority and it was to honour the head of works and his team each with an MBE, Member of the British Empire medal, they were to be in his government's first ever honours list. Secretly many in the country were happy that the head of works had the foresight and the courage to save many works of art including historic emblems of the nation.

In France many people would never get to know about the conclusions to the confidential report into the cold-blooded murder of the two police officers who were sadly killed at the flat in Paris including the families of the police officers innocently going about their duties on the fateful day they lost their lives. The Parisian Police Commandant Victor had felt as though he was being restrained by politicians stopping him finding out the truth about the circumstances surrounding his police officer's murders. Within a year he resigned his position and he retired to the south of France along with his long suffering, wife. For the people of Britain, the country would take many years to "get back to normal". At last the country had itself a Prime Minister and a government who would help steer the country back onto a true and even keel. The president of the USA was much happier knowing the people of Britain helped to topple a leftist Marxist government through the power of the ballot box. In his eyes the previous government took an honourable nation to the abys almost to oblivion. The world seemed to be a much safer place for the citizens of the world. For Sage Vasiliev's family in the Ukraine they had no idea he was found dead in a flat in France. His family in Ukraine were led to believe by the Russians of all things he was killed in combat in the Ukraine region on the Russian border, it was politics working again the Russians were doing the Ukrainian politicians dirty work and tidying up the loose ends. As such Sage would be buried in a pauper's grave and in a tiny French graveyard close to the two police officers who were killed looking for him it was ironic. What Alek and Dmytro had not realised was their intended "target" was not the man they thought he was. The Russian President did not always turn up to where he was meant to be. Security was paramount and upper most within Russia whenever it concerned the President but, in his case, there was a doppelganger someone who looked just like him, and that person was paid a lot of money to take the presidents place during many events in and around the Russian state. The real President never met the man who would often stood in for him and often put his life in danger, at many venues around Russia. Even if the, would be assassins ever got close to their intended target they would have failed in their assignment as the man they were sent to assassinate was not their intended victim? And if they did succeed in killing the man they would have been ruthlessly tracked down, hunted, and killed by the Russian security services. Before Dmytro and Alek ever got to their assignment the Ukrainian secret services "pulled" the hit and contacted Dmytro in the field ordering him to eliminate Alek it was possible the hit was called off because of political reasons., Many months later the rumours doing the rounds in Kiev was because of political reasons. "Joining the European union was cited as one reason" many in the SBU had their own conspiracy theories such as the hit was called off because the Russian president had personally contacted the Ukrainian president and he ordered him "to call off his dogs because if he didn't the Russian President would make things run smoothly between Ukraine and the European union leading to Ukraine's acceptance into the union". If not, there was a growing fear in Kiev and it was common knowledge the Russians would commit cyber warfare and would bring down the country's power grid and other of the Ukraine's utilities more importantly the supply of Russian oil to the country. Nothing more was ever said but was abundantly clear the Russians knew full well there was a "hit" squad roaming around Russia. Alek was to be the sacrificial lamb sent to the slaughter and what was very ironic about the whole situation was he Alek would be killed in the country of his birth the same country he built up so much hatred for. Each member of his family was dead and Alek's blood line had died out when he was killed. There was no one left to carry on the family blood line? His body was eventually given a decent burial what was left of it, the Russian coroner managed to extract a tiny piece of DNA from his body. It was routinely run through the states DNA databank and his DNA was matched to DNA held on the military's database it showed up as a Major Alek Petrov the FSB were immediately by the coroner's office and were informed of the discovery of Major Alek Petrov's body, but the FSB hadn't been surprised. Many weeks later in a Moscow graveyard and beside a family plot Alek's body was, laid to rest next to his parents and his brother's grave. The send-off was witnessed by a few members of the FSB and a member of Ukraine's Embassy based in Moscow. The funeral directors were paid by a mystery woman. Inside the graveyard and away from Alek's funeral and standing alone was a beautiful woman she was observing the funeral from a distance. As soon as his coffin was lowered into the ground she turned away and walked towards a black car parked within the cemetery grounds. She climbed into the car and spoke to the driver and she waited patiently until an elderly but smartly dressed man got into the same car as the mystery woman. He sat in the rear of the car next to the younger woman. "Ah Kateryna dear Alek has been laid to rest with his beloved family, he is so much happier now" the woman turned to face the old man and replied, "No we are his family me and his baby and when it is born it will bear his name his blood will course through the baby's veins in life not death". She sat with one hand on her belly. The car conveyed the pair to the Ukrainian Embassy in

Moscow. The old man and the young woman walked to the Ambassadors office. The man knocked on the door the pair were invited into the room. The Ambassador asked the man to leave the room. The man stood before her stood up and approached her he then kissed Kateryna on the cheek. "How are you my child" she replied, "not so good uncle, and what the fuck was Alek doing in bloody Russia" he replied, "ah only god knows the answer to your question my child". She hadn't believed her uncle not a word. He told her "the president has placed a king's ransom into your bank account, it is the money he feels the country owes Alek and you of course the child". She hissed at her uncle "more like blood and guilt money, what do I tell the child about what happened to its father when the child is old enough to ask"? The Ambassador replied, "tell it fuck all, now Kateryna you need to get yourself back to the Ukraine and right now, you have been granted temporary diplomatic immunity to enable you to travel to the airport and to leave the country straight away so far, the Russians have no idea who you are or linked to him in any way." She kissed her uncle goodbye and she travelled to the airport in the Embassy's diplomatic car as it headed for Sheremetyevo International Airport in Moscow. Meanwhile in Britain far away from the dirty world of Assassins and spies in Eastern Europe.

The British Prime Minister Mark Brown was extremely anxious to undo many of the policies of the outgoing government. Policies implemented to the detriment the people of Britain. Mark knew it would take at least four years to rectify the chaos left by Julien Jones's government. He hoped the public would trust him enough for him to lead the country for a second term in office. As it would only be under a second term of government, the public would start to notice the benefits of the policies his government would soon bring to the country. He needed to get the world's financial institutions to once again to believe in Great Britain by having a stable government in place and it would go a long way to gain confidence of the rest of the world. He began by forming stronger ties with the Americans and more importantly the country's president. Mark was relieved when he and his party were elected as the Prime Minister also when he found out the Americans had lifted the food embargo. It may have seemed a trivial affair to some, having the grain supply cut off, but grain provides so many basics foods such as Bread, Cereal foods and pasta to name a few. Grain is such a basic food commodity but one of the most important. For a couple of years, the country turned to food rationing not seen since the 1940's and the 1950's for many it was the first time they had experienced rationing and it wasn't something they wanted to experience again. By America having lifted the blockade and it helped to project the prime minister as a politician who was accepted by the people and many of the world leaders and he was someone they trusted and could work with. Martin invited his minister of defence and the defence chiefs to a meeting at Number 10 downing street regarding the state of Britain's Armed Forces and the state of the countries defence. During the meeting he asked the First Sea Lord, Chief of the Naval Staff, how long would it take to "get the country's nuclear submarines out to sea on operations"? The First Sea Lord replied, "sir we have been keeping the submarines ticking over in their ports, but for three years we haven't had any of the subs out on patrols at sea". The prime minister stopped him in mid sentence "all I want to know is how many subs can we put to sea right now" The First Sea Lord replied, "five subs sir and we have two that need total refits and upgrading" the PM replied, "good now get the crews ready I want them out at sea in two days is that clear"? He replied, "yes sir" but the PM wasn't satisfied at the reply he felt as though there was some reluctance "Admiral if you are not up to the task I promise you I will find someone who is up to the task do I make myself very clear and do you fully understand what I am saying"? He replied "perfectly". The PM sent a strong signal to the world, Britain was once again open for business. Three days later the Prime Minister was sat in his office he was reading through some policy documents when his phone rang he picked up the phone as he spoke a booming voice spoke "well Mr prime minister you have made me so happy, my naval people have informed me they have picked up some radio traffic and sonar data from five of Britain's nuclear submarine subs in the water and where they are where they belong it's a great display from our closest ally, by the way the Russians have pulled back from some areas of the Atlantic and the Norwegian Sea, keep it up we are impressed" Mark thanked the president and placed the phone back down onto its cradle. He picked up the secure phone and asked to be put through to the 1st Sea Lord at his office. He was a little taken aback at having the Prime Minister phoning him out of the blue, without any warning. Mark phoned him to catch the Sea Lord on the hop. Mark said, "First Sea Lord may I firstly take this opportunity to congratulate you and your various teams for the huge effort in getting the five subs out to sea". The Admiral replied, "thank you but may I also point out to you after this latest political stunt I am withdrawing the submarines". The PM spoke and he was very angry and his tone was more stern "now I thought you would say something like this, Admiral I am going to replace you as I think you have been contaminated by your previous service to the previous government, I want you to resign your post and let someone else take your position who actually wants to build the country's defence capability and for the Armed Forces to be able to hold their heads high and full of pride once more. If you will not resign I shall have no other course but to sack you myself, now do I make myself bloody clear"? there was a sheepish reply "yes sir" and the PM was very angry so much, so he slammed the phone down on the Admiral. A week later the First Sea Lord did indeed resign from the Royal Navy. A more of a go getter of a First Sea Lord was promoted into the vacant post. The five submarines were withdrawn from service only to be quickly refitted and new crews were placed onboard two of the submarines they were quickly turned around and were sent out into the open seas. The PM's action sending five nuclear submarines out to sea showed the Russians Britain meant business once again, it showed Britain's previous allies the country was once again back on track and there to take up its Defence commitments. The French were extremely happy to know a key ally was back in business. The grain from both America and Canada soon began to flood into British ports and life in the country began to slowly return to some form of normality. Mark Brown had much work to do before the country could return to a resemblance of normality. Meanwhile Julian Jones the outgoing prime minister returned to a life of what some would call normality.

Julien Jones the outgoing Prime Minister was spending much of his time writing a book all about his tenure as Prime Minister and after its publication he soon disappeared from public life and was rarely heard of again. Sometimes an outgoing Prime Minister would be honoured by being such as being made a Lord not in this case. One must shed a thought for the many ordinary people of Britain who would never get over what he and his government had reduced the country to. For those who were murdered or seriously injured by the terrorist attacks on so many village pubs and the village halls under his governments care and their protection. Since George was awarded the George Cross, for his outstanding bravery, his life soon changed and forever it was for the better. One of the national newspapers found someone to help ghost write his life story and more importantly the days leading up to the terrorist attack on his sister's village and for George his life never looked back and with the money from his book and the serialisation of the book in one of the major daily newspapers and he had taken care of his sister Mary and her family, he paid off their mortgage he also purchased a house in the next village very close to his sisters village. In London there were a few people who missed old George and his outbursts in the local pub. He employed a house clearing company to empty his bedsit he packed his prized possessions into a single back pack that was him gone to live in an idle deep in the countryside. To live a very pleasant life without any worries, certainly no money worries. Julian Jones was occasionally spotted attending various fringe Marxist rallies around the country. He crept quietly into obscurity and in some people's minds he had crept back under the stone he had emerged from in the first place. Many people thought he wasted a once in a lifetime chance to use his intelligence for the good of the country but instead he almost brought the country to its knees. Mark Brown and his government were faced with an extremely and difficult task to rectify the total mess the previous government had made of running the country into the ground it was a bit of a poisoned chalice. Mark did not assume anything in life, but he hoped the British people would give him the time he and his government required in turning the country around and make it prosperous once more. He needed to sort out the burden of tens of thousands of so called "migrants" having entered the country unfettered. The strain on the country's facilities was by now at breaking point and many of the migrants travelled from many parts of the world's war-ravaged regions and so many were suffering from battlefield wounds when they eventually arrived in the UK from Europe they had needed specialist medical care and in some of the European country's they travelled through they hadn't been treated for some of their wounds. Hence on arrival putting an immense strain on the UK's infrastructure. Many migrants travelled through many countries and they eventually ended up in Britain the Europeans were more than happy, Britain was by now out of the European union those countries leaders virtually waved the migrants through their own countries, the migrant and refugee crises wasn't their problem any more, it was Britain's. Many refugees and migrants died during their travels to get to Britain. The British government turned to the many military doctors and nurses by using military field hospitals some of the field hospitals were set up within the grounds of major trauma hospitals all around the country. The NHS also appealed for many volunteers even for doctors who were retired because the was a national crisis and as many medical professionals were needed to help cope with the massive surge of serious medical casualties. The government came up with a plan to document the tens of thousands of migrants and the refugees who recently flooded into the country. It was all because of the recent terrorist attacks the government also boosted the funding for additional resources to combat terrorism. Both MI5 and MI6 understood there were many terrorists now unaccounted for within the country who managed to get into the country without any checks being carried out whatsoever and were still unaccounted for and god knows what terrorist atrocities they were planning sometime soon? The government invested in public information ads on TV, Radio and in newspapers for the public to come forward and to report anyone or anything suspicious no matter how trivial it may seem.

From the Shadows

The government now had two big problems on their hands, one was the country's huge debt crises and the untold number of migrants having arrived into the country in such a short period of time. Including the self-inflicted terrorist threat to the country it was all due to the open doors policy and it was one of the most idiotic things a government could have done. The prime minister, Mark Brown, needed the time to get the country back on track he hoped the people of the country would give him the much-needed time to complete the massive task facing him and his government, the country was almost bankrupted after the escapades of the previous government. The American President was such a great help to the Prime Minister and more especially since lifting the food embargo. Immediately after the embargo had been lifted the people immediately noticed the benefits as much food was beginning to fill the supermarket shelves. In Paris Victor was enjoying his retirement his thoughts would sometimes wander to that horrendous day in Paris when his police colleagues were murdered in such a callous manner. The British PM, Mark, was fully aware of foreign states who were still attempting to attack the UK via cyber warfare. Cyber warfare if it was used successfully in bringing down the country's power grid be it electricity or gas. If the attackers were successful it could bring down governments and bring a country to its knees. Britain could not allow this to happen and more especially when the country had so recently been crippled by the devastating food embargo. It was imperative that Britain remained strong and be able to thwart any possible future cyber-attack. Threats from other countries was fluid and could take the form of many guises, be it fuel, food and cyber threats or attack. In Brussels Bertrand and Emile continued to drink in their favourite bar and were fully aware of the recent events in Britain. The pair hadn't been affected by any of the events in Europe, their world was sleep, eat

217

and drink. European leaders did not have any idea about Russia's recent intention of invading western Europe. NATO ministers were relieved on hearing the good news the current British prime minister was wanting to re-join the alliance. Britain was one of the more reliant and reliable member of the alliance Britain was a pivotal pin within NATO. The Americans found the British a great friend and a strong ally who could be relied upon during a crisis. The US president needed many assurances from the current British Government before he eventually lifted the food embargo. The Americans knew there were some extremely dangerous people who recently entered the UK and were still hell bent on trying to carry out terrorist attacks. The US were extremely concerned the previous UK government may have issued everyone who then freely entered the country a UK passport and if they had it would prove very difficult for the American security services to weed out any UK terrorist. Mark Brown agreed to the American security services and agreed to use the help from the Americans in routing out and arresting any terrorists still free within Britain. The President thought it best that the terrorist threat was on the Britain's soil and not American soil.

Once again it is all about politics?

Chapter 9 – The Aftermath

The previous British Prime minister, Julien Jones eventually disappeared from politics after the defeat at the last general election. His disastrous premiership with its idealistic ideas were based in the past, his government virtually bankrupted the country. His only success was the writing of his autobiography, it had limited success.   Many of his front bench members of parliament had tried without any success to obtain employment in the City of London, their reputations went before them. There hadn't been a single company in the country who would ever touch them with a barge pole, they had blotted their copy book for ever more. The American government were still extremely wary even of the latest British government and British politics, after the debacle of the previous government and the lengths America had to go to helping the United Kingdom, once again. It would taint the "special" relationship for many years to come. Britain owed a huge debt of gratitude to the people of America. Britain would have a very large bill to pay for many years to come. The only good thing to come out of the whole saga for Britain it was the country didn't end up bankrupt, if he had become bankrupt it would have been disastrous. It may not have been able to recover. The newly elected British government had to delve into the overseas aid budget, it made no sense to give it away when it was needed to help the country recover. The Prime Minister Mark Brown could not justify to the people such a large budget and watch the country struggle with the immense debt it had been left with.   The overseas aid budget was still worth billions of pounds.   The American president recently contacted the PM and in no uncertain terms told him America would not continue to assist the country financially when the overseas aid budget was still being thrown away to other countries and so America was placing immense pressure on the PM to use the budget to help fund very needy projects within the UK. It was time for some common sense to prevail and in the end it did.

It was this a sign of things to come, in other words, will the Americans exert pressure on the British government when they do not like something the British government were doing? It took many years for the country to recover from the ruinous policies of the previous government under the then Prime Minister Julien Jones's premiership. Martin Brown's government did need a second term in government and the people in the last general election voted him and his government for a second term.

The deaths of the two French police officers were over time forgotten about. All apart from their families and friends, the events during that fateful day would never be forgotten in the memories of those close to them.

In Ukraine Kateryna eventually gave birth to a baby boy and she named her son after his father Alek. The boy had a very rosy future ahead of him. He would eventually be educated at some of the best schools in Britain. He was destined to be a future leader on Ukraine he had an education some of his countrymen could only dream of.

The British government eventually came up with a drastic agricultural policy to ensure the country wasn't so reliant on any other country for the basic food crops and could survive another food shortage, it was an uphill struggle and a huge change of mindset to get the right people to take on the mammoth task of growing the crops and people to farm the animals to feed the nation, but it was a start.

Regarding the massive influx of refugee and migrants the government passed a motion in parliament to help to assist the many thousands of people who flooded the country and it was to assist many thousands of people to return to their native country. Those who did volunteer to return home were given handsome payments. It would allow those people to set up businesses or to help purchase a home for them and their families. The RAF, Royal Air Force, flew many thousands to the country of their choice. Britain's borders were by now closed. The immigration camps over in France were once again full and overflowing with Refugees and migrants.

Mark Brown's government granted even more fracking licenses. The tax revenue from the business was most welcome and at the time needy. The overseas aid budget remained on hold until the needier causes within the UK were returned to a healthy state and the country could morally and financially return to distributing aid to worthy causes overseas.

The Russians were still sabre rattling, thankfully it had been no more than that.

The Aftermath

The Chinese military expansionist dreams remained in The South China seas. It led to Australia being extremely concerned about China's ambitions within the region. America had military bases in Australia, a hangover from WWII but because of China's expansionist ideas in the region, the US deployed even more forces to the Australian bases. The world still wasn't a safe place to live in still with so many nations flexing their muscles. When would it ever stop??

Made in the USA
Columbia, SC
22 June 2018